Falling
for
Mr. Right

(book five of the Falling for Mr. Wrong series)

by Jenny Gardiner

What people are saying about Jenny Gardiner's books:

Red Hot Romeo

"Awesome". So enjoyed the romantic chemistry between the two characters. Read it non stop into the wee hours. Highly recommend this book
   -- Mrs. K

Blue-Blooded Romeo

"Another brilliant, fun read from Jenny Gardiner. The book is fun to read and I thoroughly enjoyed every word. Jenny Gardiner has put the fun back into romance books and I look forward to each book in this delightful series."
   -- Anne Blyth

"I had planned on only reading a few chapters at first but couldn't put it down. A terrific storyline, well-developed and extremely relatable characters, what's not to love?? Great read!"
   -- Samantha Reeves

Big O Romeo

"I could not put this book down. Warning don't start this book late at night as you will not want to stop reading.
    -- Di

Sleeping with Ward Cleaver

"A fun, sassy read! A cross between Erma Bombeck and Candace Bushnell, reading Jenny Gardiner is like sinking your teeth into a chocolate cupcake...you just want more."
    --Meg Cabot, NY Times bestselling author of Princess Diaries, Queen of Babble and more

Slim to None

"Jenny Gardiner has done it again--this fun, fast-paced book is a great summer read."
    --Sarah Pekkanen, NY Times bestselling author of *The Opposite of Me*

Chapter One

BEFORE a major competition, Madison Henderson felt like a boxer prepping for a showdown match, obsessively adhering to "prefight" rituals so that everything worked in her favor. First she put on her noise-canceling Bose headphones—the ones that cost about as much as a small car—so she could tune out all distractions. She had her phone loaded with super Zen music—the kind you'd hear at a spa or when you got an acupuncture treatment with a lot of rainwater and seabirds and waves crashing on the shoreline and Native American flutes—and she closed her eyes while absorbing the peaceful sounds. Anything to soothe her jangled nerves.

Next she visualized what victory looked like: how she'd win and how the audience would react to her win. And she envisioned the ten thousand dollars warming her pocket, finally giving her the chance to attend pastry school, something she'd wanted to do for years.

She wished she could wrap herself in a satin boxer's robe and have a trainer massage her shoulders, which she knew would be about as tight as a virgin's snatch by the time the night was out. Except she didn't have a trainer, so never mind that luxury. It was true when she got anxious, she scrunched her shoulders up toward her ears and always paid for it the next day with a sore neck and shoulders. Assuming she won tonight, she'd spring for a masseuse with the meager winnings to take care of that problem.

Next came the mindful self-affirmations she went over in her mind:

I am the architect of my life; I built its foundation and I choose its contents.

Today, I am brimming with energy and overflowing with joy.

I am superior to negative thoughts and low actions.

I have been given endless talents, which I begin to utilize today.

I possess the qualities needed to be extremely successful.

Creative energy surges through me and leads me to new and brilliant ideas.

My ability to conquer my challenges is limitless; my potential to succeed is infinite.

I am at peace with all that has happened, is happening, and will happen.

I'm the fucking queen of trivia.

Well, that last one wasn't necessarily as mindful a thought as the other ones, but she knew it was true, and sometimes a little excessive confidence was in order.

It was a good thing she wasn't like a baseball player, or she'd swear off shaving her legs or changing her underwear or having sex until she lost a match. And by now, she'd have some serious gorilla legs because she hadn't lost in a long time. Not to mention dirty underwear. Though thanks, but no thanks—so not her style. Maddie preferred her panties to be the super girlie girl kind and definitely clean. As far as the sex thing, well, the bummer was life had pretty much defaulted into sex-free anyhow, considering the dearth of relationships she'd been mired in for far too long, so that was a moot point. But were it a factor in her life, no way would she put an end to that to win a game. Theoretically, anyhow. After all, she did love to win.

But was trivia night merely a game? Not so much for Maddie. It was her thing, so she had a lot invested in it. And for that reason, yeah, she got super nervous before a match (okay, so nobody else called them matches but her. She recognized that was a little hypercompetitive). She reminded herself regularly that her precompetition jitters were normal—what anyone would experience before a big sparring event.

This all could seem a bit dramatic for someone bracing to compete in her local bar's trivia night. It wasn't as if she was prepping to win the Boston Marathon. Or gearing up to take the bar exam, with her future riding on it. Or ready to drill into someone's brain for delicate neurosurgery. Nevertheless, she was a big believer in being prepared and showing up as the best "you" you could be.

Besides, she freaking loved to win. Loved it. And dammit she could, too: no one stored more useless trivial knowledge in her brain than she did. Blame it on DNA, maybe. Or perhaps the fault rested at the feet of her first serious relationship, with a boy two years her senior and once the love of her life. The one that got away. Ish. More like the one she'd love to push out a second-story window if she ever saw his miserable rat fink ass again after the way he ditched her without a backward glance.

Ugh, stirring up negative thoughts about that traitor Donovan Reeves did nothing to help settle her anxiety. Maddie was keyed up, jittery, like she'd had three cups of espresso and an IV infusion of heavy-duty steroids. She needed to focus, redirect her mind to the business at hand. Yet now that Donovan had reared his unwelcome self into her psyche, her brain kept straying back to thoughts of him, unbidden—to the times they challenged each other to stupid contests over mindless factoids. The year their high school quiz team won the state championships. The hours they spent poring through Trivial Pursuit cards, throwing down the gauntlet to one another to see who would choke first.

For them, it was all about the challenge, not the knowledge. If you could call it knowledge. Challenge? Who was she kidding? It was more like foreplay: some bizarre libido-enhancing wordplay-foreplay ritual that got them crazy hot and bothered. Or maybe they were already hot and bothered, and they simply liked to play trivia quizzes. But somehow they seemed to do that all the time—the trivia games. Oh, and the sexual games as well.

Sometimes they'd even throw down a trivia challenge to decide who got to do what to the other. Hmmm. Maybe they were just weird. Oddballs, yet perfect for one another. At least that's what Maddie thought until stupid Donovan up and bailed on her right when he was leaving for college. She'd thought they would continue dating indefinitely. Instead he cut off communication and left town. And abandonment was so not her thing.

It was bad enough having had a mother who'd

walked out on her and her brother Carter when they were younger. Now, the only reason Maddie would ever want to see Donovan's face again would be to slug it (and the rest of him) for betraying her in such a cruel fashion and leaving her heart in tatters. But Donovan hadn't been back to Verity Beach in forever. She'd heard through the grapevine he was a doctor now, not that she'd asked around. When she learned through the rumor mill that he'd remained somewhere far away, she was glad. Some island in the Pacific, maybe? Or some nation at war. It didn't matter to her as long as she'd never have to encounter that miserable face of his ever again. Even if he did have a pair of sexy brown eyes that sucked you in and made you all warm and cozy and safe. As if. Make that past tense. At least now she knew what lying eyes those were all along.

She had to completely purge him from her head or thoughts of that would psych her out entirely, and she needed to win tonight. She was determined to crush the competition in the statewide trivia championships, so working—and winning—the local weekly games at pubs in the Verity Beach area to train would keep her sharp and ready for the looming competition for which she'd qualified.

Maddie took a deep breath in through her nose and exhaled through her mouth, releasing built-up tension. She repeated it a few more times. She could do this. She flipped down her car visor, switched on the lighted mirror, then spread on a little more lipstick and one more layer of mascara to highlight her sea glass-green eyes. Pulling off the ponytail holder that had contained a mass of curly dark hair, she gave her head a strong shake, turned off the ignition, and exited the car. As she approached the massive twenty-foot, three-dimensional, hook-legged pirate that stood sentry atop the roof of the Peg Leg, she nodded at the veritable patron saint of this dark, crusty old pub that had been in Verity Beach for as long as she could remember.

She grabbed the (somewhat tasteless) pirate hook door handle and entered the bar. As her eyes adjusted to the dim light inside the low-ceilinged space draped with old fishing nets that she swore still reeked of fish, she recognized her small team already seated at a table near the emcee stand set up in the center of the room. She glanced at the list of team names that had been posted for the night's competition, noticing the usual suspects: Don't Know Much About History (she always beat them handily), Just the Facts Ma'am (those guys couldn't win a competition if their lives depended on it), and finally, her team, Trivia Newton John, high scorers extraordinaire, natch. Then she noticed another group had been added to the list, one she'd not heard of before: Tequila Mockingbird. Huh. She thought she knew all the trivia teams in town. She wondered who'd spearheaded the group.

She greeted her trivia team: Olivia Singletary, who was a hostess at Red Fish Blue Fish, where Maddie's brother was head chef; Tamara Thompson, who owned a small bed-and-breakfast in town where Maddie worked; and Jesse Montgomery who did some sort of IT work that Maddie didn't even pretend to understand.

They high-fived each other and Olivia handed Maddie her usual beer—a pint draft of her favorite Shark Bite IPA, which she drank at every trivia night to keep things the same for good measure. Not that she was superstitious, but still.

"Hey, so who is this new group I see posted on the board?" Maddie said, taking a sip of her beer.

Tamara shrugged. "Tequila something or other. I have no idea. Don't recognize them." She pointed toward a guy in a blue-and-white-ticking button-down and khaki shorts whose back was to them. He was engaged in conversation with what must have been his team.

"Weird. So unexpected to have newbies out of nowhere show up like that this late in the season. Usually you hear something at least through the grapevine."

The emcee, Joey Farmiggio, announced the game was about to begin, so players settled into their seats, their pens at the ready.

This was when Maddie always made sure to aim a strategically placed cold hard stare into the eyes of her adversaries, hoping to intimidate them a little bit before they had a chance to do so to her. Sure it wasn't particularly sportsmanlike, but she was in it to win it, baby. She needed all the advantages she could muster.

Maddie turned to glance at team Tequila Mockingbird, thinking it would be best to cast her steely-eyed glare their way first, only to have her eyes meet a pair of brown ones that made her gasp.

There before her was the very man she hoped never to see again, the one she fantasized about punching in the face for years, the one who shat all over her happiness like he was a pigeon and she a random car parked beneath his roosting tail.

And he had the audacity to break out into a huge grin as their eyes locked.

What a miserable rat bastard.

Make that a terribly handsome miserable rat bastard who still made her heart skip a beat despite how much she hated him, dammit.

Chapter Two

DONOVAN Reeves had made some good decisions in his life and some bad ones. And he'd learned through his better decisions that you ultimately need to accept what you've done and move on. Life can be brutal, so you do what you can, fix what you screwed up, if possible, and don't beat yourself up too much over any of it.

He'd recently returned to his hometown of Verity Beach, in the Outer Banks of North Carolina, after many years away. First there'd been college, then medical school, then his residency in emergency medicine, and finally a stint in the Democratic Republic of the Congo, the DRC, as a doctor with Médicins Sans Frontières, known as MSF, or Doctors without Borders.

For years he'd felt a restlessness he couldn't quite extinguish, so he'd volunteered with MSF, hoping it would quell whatever unease kept him feeling on edge so much. During his many years of medical training, he figured it had more to do with lack of sleep, plus being keyed up from the constant need to learn, study, prepare, perform, and not screw up.

Med school wasn't for the faint of heart, and after years of near-drowning in his education, he figured it could easily have rendered him permanently overstressed and on edge. He'd hoped immersing himself in a different culture with people whose needs far exceeded his own—or needs he could never even fathom—would disarm his anxiousness. Maybe reducing life to its most base level would lower the intensity of his disquietude.

And boy, was he right. Often working seven days a week for months on end with the most rudimentary of medical equipment and supplies, with people whose ailments, suffering, and degrees of malnutrition were wholly unfamiliar to him certainly lifted his unease. He barely had time to brush his teeth, let alone wonder or worry about what had once kept him up at night or mentally pacing the floors by day.

Of course the flip side was working nearly a year under pretty primitive medical conditions. Children died on his watch from the most preventable of diseases like measles and cholera, which left him burned out and in need of a change of scenery. Before his stint in the Congo, he'd sought the unknown, and sure enough, he found it in a big way. He'd toiled under harsh conditions a world away from the comfortable life he'd always known. He was proud of the work he'd accomplished and hoped he'd made at least a small difference in the lives of the people he'd met in the DRC. But his brain and his body were fried, and he truly needed something to revitalize his spirit. Hopefully his mom's home cooking and the familiarity of a life he once knew would help restore some balance.

So here he was, back home, wondering if what he needed was what he'd known all along: the comforts of home, family, and friends, the very thing he walked away from years earlier in an effort to spread his wings a bit and try on a new life, one not under the thumb of his demanding father.

He'd only been back in town for a week after his debriefing with MSF in Paris. Wow, was that weird, experiencing the bright lights of Paris and the abundance of amazing food, wine, and culture after his experience in the primitive world of the DRC. There, the daily effort of life was exhausting, be it ensuring you had potable water, or eating a daily diet of bland manioc mush, or navigating your way on a motorcycle through dubious roads washed away into three-foot-deep mud pits by rainy-season deluges.

Nothing comes easy for those living in countries like the DRC—the needs are so great, the availability so minimal; life is a perpetual hardship and aspirations are low on the one hand, but the tolerance of such struggles is impressively high. Donovan figured if you don't expect things to get better, you accept what you have and learn to live with it as best you can. For the people he grew to love while living there, this was, of course, all they ever knew, so despite the direst of living conditions, each day they greeted him with a smile and kind words. It taught him much about how best to live.

Which brought him back to why he'd found himself sitting in this dingy pirate-themed bar complete with scantily clad beer-wench-style cocktail waitresses, gearing up for a game of trivia that felt, frankly, incredibly trivial after all he'd been through this past year. He'd be lying to himself if he didn't admit the true reason he'd come back to Verity Beach: he hoped to make amends with his childhood sweetheart, a girl he'd loved deeply but whose heart he broke for her own good more than a decade ago. He'd hated to do it but knew (or thought he knew) he'd made the right choice—egged on by his domineering father, who had put such pressure on Donovan to follow in his footsteps and pressed him to cut all ties before leaving Verity Beach. What was an obedient son to do but listen to his father?

Donovan had done a little forensics work upon his return home, got the low-down on Maddie Henderson's life, learned with great relief no man was occupying a spot in it, and mapped out a way to at least try to ingratiate himself back into her world. That is, if she didn't beat him up or bludgeon him to death or maybe grab that gigantic pirate's cutlass on the wall over there and shish kebab him with the thing. To be honest, she had every right to. And if he were Maddie, there's no way he'd even speak to him, let alone reconcile. So he could hardly blame her if she refused to acknowledge him.

But a man could hope. And one thing that Donovan learned over the past year was that human beings could live through a lot with a little bit of hope.

"What the ever-loving fuck are you doing here?"

Upon hearing that voice that instantly quieted the entire bar, something inside him ached at the sound after so many years.

But then his head registered the words she'd uttered, and his heart sank a bit.

It seemed maybe hope was an overrated emotion after all.

Chapter Three

IT was one thing not to be superstitious about changing your underwear when you're on a winning streak. Or even the no-leg-shaving bit. No harm, no foul, not losing sleep over that transgression. No need for 100 percent consistency in your daily habits when you're on a roll.

But this—*this!*—was beyond the pale. That miserable, traitorous, rat-fink-of-an-ex (not to mention first love) was going to throw her off her game so badly she'd lose everything—the whole enchilada—because he showed up to drop a bomb on her like this.

How dare he? The very man who upheaved her life back when she was young and gullible and predisposed to deep pangs of betrayal and occasional panic attacks (like the ones she'd suffered when her mother left) showed up as though it were nothing, and worse still, he was armed to challenge her on an opposing trivia team?

She would simply not stand for this.

She squinted and stared at him hard, willing a bolt of lightning to fire from her pupils and maybe lance his heart, so he'd end up a sizzling ashen heap on the floor of the Peg Leg. Yet damn him, if he didn't attempt to disarm her rage with that quick nod he was so good at— the one that, coupled with his crooked grin, highlighted the adorable fucking dimples in his cheeks while showcasing the dazzling white, straight teeth she'd wanted to punch out of his mealy mouth. Well, it just about slayed her.

"Maddie," he said, reaching out a hand to shake hers while extending the other arm, which she took to mean in case she was willing to hug him for old time's sake (she wasn't). "It's been awhile." She stuck her hands in her pockets rather than capitulate to his peace offering.

You could practically hear a clock tick in the room, what with the silence that hung between them.

She glanced at her watch and nodded. "Some people might call it awhile. To be precise, it's more like ten years, eight months, and fourteen days, give or take a couple." She crossed her arms, her jaw set. "Others would call that more than a decade. Some, even, an entire generation." She decidedly did not accept the olive branch of a handshake he was attempting. She wasn't going to let this skunk get off easily. Wait a minute—she wasn't going to let him get off at all. He'd made his bed—without her in it—and now he could fester in it.

Oh, but then she thought about the last time she was in bed with him, and it sent a pang of longing through that part of her lower belly, that betraying, double-crossing bit right down near her uterus that would sell her down the damned river for one more quickie with the man. Because *dayum*, she still remembered how good he was in bed and the magic he worked on her with his mouth and his—oh God, she needed to focus. Donovan betrayed her. He broke her heart. He was her very own Benedict Arnold.

"Look, Maddie, I know this isn't the right time or

place but—" He ran his fingers through his soft brown waves.

"Gee, ya think?" She shook her head. "A lifetime ago, you blew me off out of nowhere and left me racked with sadness so great I barely got out of bed for months. Now, when I've finally forgotten about you—I mean completely forgotten about you, right down to the way you always pause before saying something serious and close your eyes as if you're trying to think of the best way to present your words, dammit—then you show up here on my turf, in my domain, and impose yourself as if you belong here? As if I would have the most remote interest in even speaking to you?"

Donovan paused, closing his eyes. And she wanted to smack him. Of course he did this—all the time. She used to think it was such a charming characteristic, trying to be sure he was being evenhanded and thoughtful and deliberative before he spoke. Now it made her want to scream.

"Mads," he said, taking a deep breath. "We have a lot to talk about. A lot. I have plenty of apologizing to do. And I understand if you aren't interested in hearing me out. But I wanted you to know I'm back, so you didn't get caught off guard hearing it from someone else."

She squinted. "Oh, so instead I get caught off guard when I'm prepping for a competition. Does that make it better for you, doing it that way?"

He held up his hands. "Look, I'm not here to cause you any trouble or stress you out or pick at old wounds." He looked around the bar, his arms outstretched. "I'm here to blow off some steam. I thought it might be fun to try to test out my rusty skills and see if I still have it in

15

me."

Maddie dusted her hands off as if wiping away any responsibility for his presence. "Fine. You want to blow off some steam? Be my guest. It makes no difference to me. I'll make like you're not here. Like it's been for ten-plus years." She turned around and pulled out her chair and plopped herself down into it. "Joey—let the games begin."

It's amazing how much concentration it takes to pretend you're not focusing on someone when you can't help but focus on them. Concentration that Maddie should've been using to ensure a big win. But she found herself obsessing on how to one-up him with her answers. Which was stupid. She merely needed to answer things correctly and move on.

To hell with Donovan. Even if he looked amazing. He'd filled out over the years. No longer a scrawny teenager, now he was taller, his chest had filled out, and his shoulders were broader. He'd only gotten better looking over the years, which sucked. She'd hoped he would have sprouted warts all over his face and by now be sporting a big old beer belly, maybe a missing tooth or two.

"Mads," Olivia said, tapping her pen on the table. "I know you know this answer. We've had the question before, but I can't for the life of me remember it."

"The color of the Uzbekistan flag from top to bottom." Maddie bit her lip. "Crap. I know this."

She wrote down her answer. "You all good with this?" She held up the card with her response: blue, white, red.

The rest of her team shrugged and nodded, so she handed it to the emcee, ignoring Donovan, with whom she crossed paths on the way to the table.

"The colors are: blue, white and green," Joey announced as he took a swig of his beer. "And the points go to Tequila Mockingbird, the only team to get it right."

Maddie's eyebrows strained toward her chin she was so pissed. It only annoyed her more to see Donovan's team high-fiving him and patting him on the back. Clearly he was the one with the answer. She tried to shrug it off and move on.

"Moving on to the 'Who Am I?' round," Joey said, discarding a notecard and holding up another close to his face so he could read it. "This person ruled a Central African country for more than thirty years. He was known for his ubiquitous fur hat, fashioned from leopard pelt."

Crap. She was so bad at African history. So darned many countries to know about and constantly changing dictators. The only thing she could think of was Idi Amin, but he was East Africa. She stole a glance over at Donovan, who was in deep conversation with his team, everyone nodding their heads as he jotted down their response. God, she could practically see the wheels in his head turning and darn it, it got her so hot and bothered. The man was a freaking fount of knowledge and thinking about how they used to brainstorm together followed by super-hot bouts of sex where they couldn't strip each other's clothes off fast enough made her squirm in her seat.

What the hell? He'd gotten two questions she'd failed to answer correctly and it was making her panties wet? She was a veritable Pavlov's dog... as though she were one of those people from a horror movie who has two completely different personalities—in her case, one that made her want to kill Donovan and the other that made her want to fuck him. Right about now it was a toss-up as to which of her personalities was going to win. It might come down to the bonus round, dammit.

Chapter Four

WELL, this wasn't quite how he'd hoped things would go. He'd imagined maybe Maddie had grown up and moved on, forgiven him for his youthful transgressions and buried the hatchet, but instead, it seemed as if she was waiting to plant that blade right into his skull. For chrissake, it had been ten years. Wasn't there some statute of limitations on anger, resentment, and bitterness?

He pondered that a second and realized he was still ticked at his father for pretty much everything, not the least of which was coercing a gullible younger version of himself to bail on Maddie "for her own good." What a stupid fuck he was to believe his father had his or her best interest at heart. He was a manipulative son of a bitch and he'd always been that; why would Donovan have ever imagined he would do the right thing?

And here it was all these years later, and he was paying the price for it. He had to accept that it was likely too late to make amends, that he'd broken her heart so badly it was irreparable, and that Maddie was perhaps what had been missing in his life all these years. It was all too little, too late.

On a side note, he had, however, discovered it was

surprisingly fun and relaxing to be back in the trivia world. His life had been riddled with seriousness for so long he couldn't have imagined space in it for useless nothings. But here he was thoroughly enjoying himself and finding it near impossible to not blurt out the answer to every question. After all, he needed to give his team a chance to shine.

Unfortunately it had become clear that Maddie wasn't digging his presence—first because it was him, and second because his team was kicking ass. She always was a sore loser. But it wasn't doing him any favors to beat her, either. It would only be another nail in the coffin of any possibility of rekindling their romance. Ugh. He refused to cheat, and it would be cheating to not answer a question so she could win the point. That was lame. He couldn't do it.

"What is the fortieth element on the periodic table?" Joey shouted out to the audience.

Donovan rolled his eyes. "Are you kidding me?" he said to his team. "With the number of science classes I took purely in anticipation of going to medical school, I had that puppy committed to memory by the time I was in my second year of college." He pulled out the pen he'd tucked behind his ear. "Anyone want to hazard a guess before I write this answer down?"

He looked around at the two women and one man he'd enlisted during happy hours to join forces as a team but was met with a pout, a frown, and a grimace.

"Zirconium," he said as he jotted down the answer, slowly enunciating each syllable as he wrote the word.

"Good job," Mimi said. Wait. Was her name Mimi? Or was it Jeannie? He'd barely committed his team members' names to memory because once Maddie had entered the bar, all other people had instantly faded into the background. And here he thought she'd been beautiful in high school—those bewitching green eyes could get him to do pretty much anything. And thinking about that tumble of dark curls he used to love to tangle his fingers in, especially when he was buried deep inside her, made him hard. But now, she looked even more breathtaking, if that was possible. She'd transformed from girl to woman, and he couldn't help but stare (only when she wasn't looking) at her shapely curves, amazing tits, and grab-worthy ass that he couldn't wait to get his hands on. That is if he was ever going to get his hands on them. Clearly that was not a fait accompli.

"We're going to be taking a fifteen-minute break so everyone can fill up their drinks, hit the ladies' room, whatever suits your fancy," Joey said as he collected cards from everyone. He paused for a moment, reading the answers to each one. "Team Tequila Mockingbird goes into halftime with a strong lead. The rest of you can spend your break boning up on potential answers," he said with a laugh.

Donovan could hear his team cheering and whistling loudly. Which was all fine and good, except that he feared a win against Maddie would ultimately mean a big fat notch in the loss column for him, at least as far as wooing her back was concerned. Hell, wooing her back was awfully premature anyhow. Getting her alone in the same room would be a start. He knew the only reason she was sharing the air in here with others was that she had no choice if she wanted to play the game.

She stormed off down a back hallway, a dour look

on her face, and he decided to pursue her. If she was leaving because of him, well, he didn't want that on his shoulders. He'd rather forfeit and leave trivia night to her, so he'd tell her himself.

He noticed a sign for the bathrooms down a flight of stairs and took the steps two at a time to try to catch up to her. Too late—by the time he got to the bottom, she was nowhere to be found. It took him a minute for his eyes to adjust to the dimly lit basement. He paced the tile floor, hoping she'd gone into the bathroom and would be out in a minute. He contemplated going into the ladies' room to be sure but decided that would likely tick her off. On a good day, your average woman hates to have men looming when they have to pee.

He stopped pacing and leaned against the wall around the corner from the ladies' room, tucking his hands into the pockets of his shorts, lifting a bent knee, and pressing his foot to the wall. When he heard the door creak open, he craned his neck to see if it was her. Sure enough there she was, radiant in that cute pink-and-blue sundress with the spaghetti straps, her nipples standing at attention thanks to the air conditioning blasting downstairs. He had no idea how he was going to restrain himself from acting like old times and going right up to her and enveloping her in his arms. Except that he heard her sniffle and noticed her dabbing her eyes, which instantly kicked his protective instincts into overdrive, not even allowing him to overthink his next move.

"Mads?" he said in a quiet voice.

She gasped as she turned. "Donovan." Her eyes were wide open. "Don't scare me like that."

"I'm sorry, Maddie. I wanted to check on you

because you seemed upset. Are you okay?"

She rolled her eyes. "Am I okay? Are you kidding me? You show up here—unbidden, mind you—like some apparition, intent on haunting me. Even though I've done everything in my power to get far, far away from you. And yet here you are." She paused, pointing at him, her arm sweeping from his head to his feet. "Determined to resurrect all the hurt and pain and sadness—"

Donovan stepped forward and reached for her, pulling her toward him, pressing her head to his chest and burying his fingers in her thick hair as she began to sob. He traced lazy circles along her back with his other hand and made quiet shushing sounds to try to comfort her as he softly scratched her scalp. Sheesh, the last thing he thought would happen was an emotional meltdown. Apparently ten years wasn't enough for her to extricate him from her psyche.

"And then you show up here, looking like you do," she said between gasping sobs, "and then you go and answer all the questions. It's bad enough you get them all right, but then, but then, oh, damn you, Donovan. You know what that always did to me. And here I am hating every cell of your body and instead my body is betraying me by lapsing into ten years ago and wanting to straddle you and—"

He could barely believe his ears. Straddle him? Had she said that? His mind searched for all sorts of words that sounded like straddle: rattle, battle, cattle, tattle. Ugh, maybe she did want to battle him. That would be unfortunate. Clearly tattle wasn't the word he'd heard—after all, who would she tell? And no heifers were involved in this situation. He supposed he'd rattled her.

She must've said that. But shit, he could not get the image of her straddling him out of his brain—his useless pea brain that seemed to have two settings: dick on and dick off, and right now, with the idea of her wanting to straddle him, he was seriously in dick-on mode.

He softly lifted her head and pulled her face toward his, a questioning look in his eyes. He needed her permission to go any further. The last thing he wanted was for her to accuse him of forcing himself on her.

He didn't have to wait long. No sooner had he fixed his gaze on hers than she reached out and planted her mouth over his as she draped her arms over his shoulders, then jumped up and wrapped her legs around his waist: the next best thing to straddling.

Permission granted.

He closed his eyes against the surge of emotions surfacing inside him. During those long, lonely nights in the DRC, when he would sometimes fantasize about reuniting with Maddie while he stroked himself to climax, it wasn't anywhere near as good as this: her breasts pressed to his chest so close that he could feel her taut nipples, which was making him crazy. And her crotch rubbed against his thickening cock, making him still crazier, with the most minimal amount of fabric separating the two.

They both gasped for air as they kissed long and hard, their tongues tangling, their teeth smashing together in the urgency of the moment. He pressed his cock toward her warm center, wondering—hoping, desperately—if she was already wet for him. There was a time when he'd have asked her out loud. They loved to talk dirty to each other back then. But did he dare?

One of his hands kept shifting, tracking a drunkard's path all over her body, since he couldn't decide what he needed to touch the most. But the other, the one that was supporting her bottom, was so close to her sweet spot, he wrestled with whether to take his chances and sneak a feel. When Maddie moaned into his mouth, he became so aroused he had no choice but to shift the silky fabric of her dress away and slide his fingers beneath the edge of her panties, finding her slick and warm.

"Oh fuck, baby, you're so wet for me. I can't tell you how many times I've thought about your soaking-wet pussy spread wide open for me to slide into." He couldn't believe he was saying these things to Maddie, who thirty minutes ago was as off-limits as your best friend's kid sister. He said a little prayer of thanks that she wasn't related to any of his buddies.

He trailed kisses from her mouth to her chin, then along the column of her throat, lifting her enough to be able to lean deep and drag his tongue along her breast, which he'd quickly exposed by shifting the edge of her dress for easy access. Fastening his mouth over her nipple, he drew a long, hard suck on it, eliciting a low groan from her. She'd leaned her head against the wall that half-supported her while she remained wrapped around his waist.

Donovan slid three fingers beneath the leg of her panties, tracing along her slick core and around her swollen clit as her breathing intensified. Hell, so did his—he worried he'd pass out from hyperventilating. She rhythmically pressed herself against him, urging his fingers on, and he slid one, then two, then three inside her channel then withdrew them, mimicking what he wished he was doing with his dick.

"Oh my God, Donovan, you always did that so well." She panted heavily in between moans.

"What did I do well?" He sucked harder on her nipple, then bit down on it till she squealed.

"This. Finger fucking me. Sliding your fingers deep inside me like that."

"That's because your pussy is swollen and wet. I want to get it nice and ready for me to spread it wide with my hard cock."

Maddie thrust her hips harder toward Donovan, each time forcing herself against his throbbing dick. Shit, he was going to have wet marks on his fly by the time they finished here. Good thing he could pull his shirt out to hide the telltale signs. He didn't even care at this point. All that mattered was here he was, back to where he wanted—needed—to be, with the girl he'd been dreaming of for so many years.

His lips nudged away the fabric covering her other breast, and he made quick work of that one as well, feasting on her nipple with strokes of his tongue, nips of his teeth, and hard suckles that he was sure she could feel all the way to her pussy.

"You can feel that, can't you, Mads?" he said as he pulled hard on her nipple with his mouth. "You always used to tell me how you could feel me sucking you right down to your clit."

"Oh God. Don't stop. I can feel it starting inside me. I'm gonna come." Her hips had gone wild, gyrating against him, forcing his fingers deep inside her.

"Come all over my fingers, baby. And then I'm gonna make you lick your juices off of them." Maddie shouted out his name as she momentarily went still, then her body trembled as her pussy convulsed around his fingers.

Donovan wanted nothing more than to unzip his fly and quickly press his cock into her wet center, but this was all so completely unexpected he was almost afraid to dare do so. It was one thing to pleasure her, but another to have permission to enter her body. As he wrestled with the boner of the century causing him pain at this point, and whether it was appropriate to ask permission, the decision was made for him.

"Maddie?" It was a voice coming from the top of the staircase. Shit. The stupid game. No doubt her team was missing her and sent out a member on a search-and-rescue mission. Dammit.

Well, at least that gave him an excuse to let her gain some ground, pointwise. He was going to be stuck down here trying to calm down this killer erection at least for the duration of the Novelty Round. And for him it seemed the bonus question would be this: was this a novelty? Or could he assume that he and Maddie had officially reunited, this time, if he had any say in it, for good?

Chapter Five

FUCK to the fuckety fuck. What the hell have I done?

Maddie shuddered in the aftermath of the best orgasm she'd had in ages—make that the only orgasm she'd had in ages. At least one at the hands of a man. So she hadn't imagined it, that Donovan had always worked magic with his mouth and fingers? He was every bit as good as ever, if not better. Still, she didn't even want to think about how practice makes perfect. He'd had ten years to fine-tune his sexual prowess at the hands—or naked bodies—of countless women. The thought of it made her want to weep. It was bad enough he'd simply up and abandoned her. But to think he then willy-nilly had sex with other random women? Why them and not her? How selfish.

In the middle of relishing his tongue against hers, his mouth on her nipple, his fingers in her pussy, she'd lost sight of what his abandonment meant on many levels. He had mistreated her and no doubt moved on to glibly sleep around with hundreds of women. Plus, she'd likely denied herself good sex all these years because damn, even though she'd slept with a couple of guys in the intervening years, none could hold a candle to Donovan. He knew how to handle a woman's body. The others?

Not so much.

Good God, she'd allowed herself to get sex-drunk. What a bonehead. She'd been a heartbeat away from truly sealing the deal by letting him press his cock into her body. And lordy, how she'd wanted to feel him inside her. It would have felt like home to her. Yet that could not happen. No way, no how. Once burned, twice ready to lop off his johnson. Now came the sexual hangover part, and she needed to fix this, stat. She could no sooner let this happen again with Donovan than she could marry a dolphin. Both were unnatural occurrences that could never happen in the real world. But how to extricate oneself from this particularly awkward moment?

So it was with incredible good fortune she heard Olivia calling out her name from the top of the stairs.

"Oh, crap," she whispered, quickly dismounting the man as she straightened her panties and gave her dress several appropriate tugs in either direction to make sure all relevant body parts were no longer exposed. "I'm coming, Liv!"

Donovan shot her a look from beneath hooded lids, the one that said what they both knew: that she'd already come, with a spectacular bang, and damn, was it ever worth the wait.

She ran her fingers through her curls and wiped any evidence of kissing from her lips. Although with her luck, the razor burn would linger as a haunting reminder of this unplanned-for event.

"Uh, this," she said, pointing a finger at him and then at herself and back at him. "I, um, got carried away. That shouldn't have happened. I think you understand why."

There was this tiny part of her, the same part that

didn't step on ants and carefully picked up wasps that got trapped indoors and tossed them back outside rather than smashing them with a fly swatter, that felt kind of bad. His face fell, and he looked so disappointed. She told herself that more than likely he was only hoping to get his rocks off, and he was bummed to have been thwarted. Oh well, that's why God gave him a pair of hands. Maybe he'd divert to the men's room and finish things off, so she could get back upstairs and win some points.

"Look, Maddie." Donovan scrubbed his face with his hand. The very hand that had been making her super happy two minutes earlier. Oy. She needed to stop thinking about that. "I was hoping that maybe we could talk some more. About... things."

She shook her head. "Seriously, Donovan. No." She held up her hands as if turning away dessert. "This was a crazy—and I mean *crazy*—lapse in judgment on my part. I can't for the life of me imagine what I'd been thinking." Oh, maybe that something about Donovan Reeves still held her in sway, despite herself. That even though she held on to a veritable trash heap piled high with resentment toward him, there was no denying that he was gorgeous and still got her juices flowing—literally, oy vey—by demonstrating the breadth of his knowledge, first, and then his sexual prowess, second. What a weirdo she was to get turned on by a guy whose mind contained excessive amounts of useless trivial knowledge. Maybe she needed to seek out therapy to resolve that issue.

Donovan crossed his hands over his heart. "I totally get your reluctance to even talk to me." He leaned forward. "And I'm pleasantly surprised at your lapse in judgment. I hope it means that while you despise me, maybe you have room in your heart to not hate me."

She rolled her eyes. "It's not that I hate you." She shook her head. "Well, actually, it is that I hate you. You left me. You abandoned me. You did the very thing my mother did to me, including never once looking back, exactly like her. You belong in the pantheon of Jerks Who Broke Maddie's Heart and Made Her Unable to Trust."

"Mad? We need you." Olivia called out in a sing-song voice.

Maddie dusted off her hands, leaving this episode behind her in the process.

"Look, I've gotta go." She turned to head up the stairs.

Donovan reached out and grabbed her shoulder. "Please. Think about it. At the very least you deserve to hear me out."

"Ten years too late, D. Ten years too late."

She quickly mounted the steps, not turning to glance behind her. Her heart couldn't take stepping on an ant, even if maybe that insect deserved it.

For the rest of the evening, Maddie tried hard not to look at Donovan, but it was near impossible to do so. Especially when he leaned his head in with those two women on either side of him to discuss their answers.

She wasn't one for violence, yet something about that scene made her want to get into a hair-pulling girlfight with those chicks merely because they looked all swoony and googly-eyed at him. Who the hell did they think they were to have that intimacy with him? Of course she wasn't interested in examining why she'd experienced a much higher degree of intimacy with him earlier in the evening and yet made the decision not to continue down that path. Even though her libido was chastising her at this very moment for that self-defeating choice.

Luckily Donovan had remained in the basement for the better part of two rounds of play, which meant Maddie's team was ahead by a comfortable lead. They'd now entered the bonus round, and if they answered this question correctly, Trivia Newton John would win.

"What year was the first Soccer World Cup?" Joey said, then repeated the question. "Was it 1890, 1910, or 1930?"

Crap. Maddie hated the sports questions. This was going to be left to pure guessing. She no sooner knew this answer than she knew the secret to happiness.

"Okay let's think this through you guys," she said to her team. "I can't imagine they had normal soccer balls way back in the late-nineteenth century, you know? Or even the early-twentieth century. They wouldn't have been blown up with air. They'd have been stuffed with rags and be all lumpy. So I'm taking an educated guess and going for 1930. What do you think?"

Olivia waved her hand. "Dude. They've been playing soccer for eternity. Plus wasn't there that famous cease-fire in the trenches during the First World War on Christmas Day when soldiers from all sides quit fighting and played a soccer match? Which is weird anyhow, but still. It has nothing to do with the ball being lumpy—clearly they were playing with lumpy balls for centuries. However, I'm going to go with 1930 also, simply because it was between two world wars, so maybe it was a good time to do something international like that."

Maddie glanced around at the rest of the group. "Anyone have strong convictions about this?"

They all shrugged.

"Okay, then, we'll go with 1930."

When prompted, Maddie carried their answer up to Joey. As she turned to walk back to her table, Donovan passed by her, brushing his arm against her breast. It was as if he'd lit a match to her skin, which instantly got her heart racing. How on earth was she going to resist this man?

The teams waited while Joey checked all the votes and then he made a hand drumroll on the table. "The answer is 1930. Which means, to the victors go the spoils—Trivia Newton John, come up to claim your prize money."

Maddie held her fist in the air, then jumped up and clapped, hugging her teammates, as the rest of the players in the room had already returned to drinking their beers. It was obvious they didn't take it all as seriously as she did. With caution, she glanced out of the corner of her eye to the table where Donovan and his team sat, hoping to cop a glimpse into his reaction and then, d'oh, he caught her stealing a glance and gave her a big wink. Urgh. He was so not supposed to see her doing that. This was her cue to get the hell out of the Peg Leg before a certain person made his way over to her. She couldn't run the risk of succumbing to round two with said person who possessed warm brown eyes that crinkled at the corners when he laughed, which he was doing right now with his posse of sycophants.

She leaned over to her friends, who were chatting about some friend of theirs who was getting married in a couple of weeks. "Hey, I'm going to slip out of here," she said. "I've got to get up early in the morning. You understand."

Olivia squinted. "Oh. So it's not anything to do with trying to avoid that gorgeous man from Tequila Mockingbird who happened to be downstairs when you were down there for an extended period?"

Maddie rolled her eyes. "Please. That man means nothing to me."

But the truth was for a long time he'd meant everything to her. And now she had to figure out a way to make sure he never meant anything to her ever again. Even if the sex was still amazing.

Chapter Six

MADDIE had a passive-aggressive form of revenge to avoid overt confrontation, and it involved sharp pins and pliable voodoo dolls. It started when she was a kid and her mother up and abandoned her and her brother Carter. She was eight at the time, which is a bad time to lose a mother. Not that there's any good time. And not that she was much of a mother when she was around. It wasn't like she was baking cupcakes and showing up at soccer practice. She tended to sleep a lot and drink too much and fight with her father too often. If Maddie were honest, she'd admit it wasn't the healthiest of environments to grow up in, and in some ways her mother's absence wasn't a horrible thing. That said, with her father staying behind, the air in their household remained a bit toxic. He didn't do much to help bind the family together other than forcing her and Carter to unite against him or try to save him, which never stuck.

Anyhow, the voodoo-doll practice came about when she was simmering with rage over her mother months after she failed to return, and Maddie picked up a small stuffed doll that her mom had given her one time, found a straight pin in a kitchen drawer, and stuck it hard, right into the heart of the doll. While she did it, she whispered out loud, "Take that, Suzy Henderson." Because she wasn't sure if there was a particular type of incantation one should chant when trying to voodoo someone into terrible pain. Maddie had hoped that pain was smack-dab in her mother's heart. She deserved that at the very least.

Her mother's absence—and its impact on her—had been such a defining characteristic of her childhood, it came as a punch to the gut when Donovan, the day before he was to leave for college, pulled a runner, much like her mama. Only Donovan had the balls to screw her, literally, before he screwed her. At the time, it had been a much more tender occurrence. She didn't know he was never going to show the whites of his eyes in her presence again. The moment was bittersweet. They both knew he'd be leaving for college in twenty-four hours. How could it not be traumatic, knowing that every touch, every kiss, every everything was going to have to last for a while, at least until he came home for fall break?

They both made it last as long as possible, and when Donovan slipped out of Maddie's basement bedroom in the wee hours of the night, she was already crestfallen that in a few short hours, she'd not see him for ages. They'd been dating since she was in ninth grade, and to say she'd fallen madly in love with him was a grotesque understatement. With Donovan, she at last had someone who loved her, truly loved her. Not because he had to, which was probably the deal with her mother and father. And sure Carter loved her, but again, it wasn't as though he chose to be her brother, so what else was he going to do?

On the contrary, Donovan chose her—he didn't have to want her, but he did. He didn't have to love her, but he did. Until apparently, he didn't.

That next day, the day he was leaving for a college that was eight states away, she tried to reach him to say goodbye, only to have her calls and text messages go unanswered. At first, she feared something horrible had happened to him. It was the only logical reason for him to have gone dark on her like that. But the next day, his father answered the phone when she called, and he couldn't have been more heartless.

"Look, Madeleine," he said, not even bothering to know that her given name was Madison. Even though she was really Maddie, dammit.

"My name is Madison."

"Okay, Madison."

"But I want to be called Maddie."

"Fine. Whatever. Maddie. Donovan's left for school, and I know he decided it best to put some distance between the two of you. Surely you can understand that. He's got a whole new world in front of him, and you don't want him to be held back because you're still clinging to childish ideas about romance. Donovan would prefer a clean break so that he can start fresh, meet some girls his age, and focus on his academics. Med school isn't going to happen without his making some sacrifices, you know. So do him a big favor and let him go. Don't make it harder for him. I'm sure he feels guilty enough for going away, but I also know he's ready to move on without you."

Needless to say, after she cried till she likely hit a point of dehydration, she dug up some fabric and stuffing and a needle and thread and stitched up a custom Mr. Henderson voodoo doll that she stuck full of sharp pins for years afterward. On a good day, she'd never liked that guy and after that? She'd likely have stuck pins into his very flesh had she ever come face-to-face with him again, the fucker.

If she had time on her hands, she'd knit a doll. The very motion of knitting was calming, but tonight, she had a sense of urgency. In a pique of déjà vu, she rifled through a pile of fabric scraps, dug up some fiberfill, found the needle and thread, and whipped together a new voodoo-doll version of Donovan Henderson. The one she'd made of him all those years ago had worn threadbare, so she eventually got rid of it. That night she fell asleep stitching together his side seams and never had a chance to stick it to him good before she drifted into unsettling dreams.

She dreamed that Donovan and her mother had shown up to celebrate her eighteenth birthday. Her mom had on a party hat, and Donovan had one of those cardboard blow horns like the ones you use on New Year's Eve. Maddie was so confused why they would be there at all, but even more so why they would be together with her. Neither cared about her. It would be crazy for them to want to be kind to her.

And then her father came out, dressed in a business suit—something she'd never seen the man in ever— carrying her birthday cake with sparklers shooting those fizzy jolts of flames and sparks, and they all joined their voices to sing a rousing round of "Happy Birthday." A sense of peace, the type she'd never known before, descended over her as this dream unfolded. It was as if nothing was like it was and now she knew everything was completely different—better. Carter was there, arm in arm with his girlfriend Jamie, and everyone was beaming at Maddie, whose dog—but she didn't own a dog!—was curled in a deep sleep on her lap. Never had she wanted a dog more than at this moment to punctuate the perfect picture of her life completely.

So when her alarm went off at six the next morning and she woke up to her real life, the one with no mom, a shitty dad, and a heartbreaker of an ex-boyfriend who didn't count, she heaved a sigh and a small tear trickled from the corner of her eye. She definitely needed to get a dog.

Chapter Seven

IT pained Donovan to throw the trivia match her way by default... but not too much. While he preferred to win—like it or not, all those years of medical school and residency had reinforced his desire to be right—if he'd won, all bets about reuniting with Maddie would be off forever.

This way it at least let him bide his time while he figured out an actual plan of action. His original plan, hoping for the best and seeing what happened, had backfired. Well, not totally. He did, after all, have a good ten or so minutes with his hands under her panties and his mouth on her succulent breasts, so that wasn't a total loss.

He lay in bed thinking back to the night before, that moment when Maddie leapt onto him, her legs wrapped around his waist, her lips planted on his. Jesus, thinking about it made him hard all over again. He'd already taken care of that urge twice—once in the men's room at that ridiculous pirate bar last night and once when he got home. He was fully prepared to go for round three, except he could smell bacon on the stove and knew any minute his mother would call him down for breakfast. The last thing he needed was to have her walk in on him while he had his dick in his hand.

Instead he got up, took a quick shower, threw on a pair of shorts, then went downstairs to greet his mom.

"Smells delicious, Mom." He gave her a big squeeze. It was interesting—when his father was alive, his mother seemed to live in the shadows of his larger-than-need-be presence. But now that he'd been gone a few years, his mother seemed so much more open. Used to be he'd put his foot down and she meekly acceded. With her shoulders pulled back, she stood a little taller, maybe relishing her freedom without his dad, who had a habit of sucking the air out of a room.

"What's on the agenda today, mama bear?" He held up his plate to his mother who was piling it high with bacon and eggs and grits.

"I have a luncheon with the hospital women's group. You remember I was very involved with that when your father was still alive."

He nodded. "You doing it because you want to, or because Dad would have expected you to?"

She shrugged. "Maybe a little of both? It's nice not having to be the chairwoman for every damned fundraiser someone proposes. Your father would expect that of me. But to be honest, I have a group of friends there who've been doing it as long as I have, so it's nice to catch up with them. What've you got planned?"

He leaned back and scrubbed his bare chest. "I should be doing something useful, but what I want to do is absolutely nothing."

She leaned over and kissed the top of his head. "Sweetie, I'd say you've earned that. Why don't you take the day and relax on the beach? Maybe bring along a book. We've got some chairs in the garage if they're not too rusted out. Maybe call your sister and see if she'll join you."

"Ma, Sarah's got two kids."

"Yes, but kids love the beach!"

"Of course they do. But if there are kids involved, that kills the idea of relaxing on the beach."

She shook her head as she sat down across from him at the breakfast table. "Honestly, you go from so hyperinvolved in life to wanting no attachments whatsoever. Speaking of attachments… I heard you making some calls about Maddie yesterday. Did you find out anything?"

His eyes grew wide. "How could you hear me? I was upstairs in my room!"

She lowered her eyes. "Silly boy. I hear everything through the vent."

He arched a brow. "Everything?"

She shook her head. "Some things are best left unsaid. But what about Maddie?"

He sighed and stretched his legs out on the seat that used to be reserved exclusively for his father. He relished putting his feet up on it. Even tyrants eventually faded away. "Mom, I was stupid. I let Dad dictate his terms to me. I didn't even think twice about it. Well, maybe twice but no more. I just capitulated to his demands. And the last thing she wants is anything to do with the likes of me."

She leaned over and brushed a hank of hair away from his eyes. "That's what you think. And maybe that's what she thinks. But what I do know is this: you're single and have never been in a serious relationship since her.

And she's single and has never been in a serious relationship since you."

He squinted. "How on earth do you know that?"

She patted his hand. "It's a small town. And I've managed to keep tabs on Maddie over the years. You two were together for a long time, honey. I grew to love her like a daughter."

"Then why did you let Dad do that to me?" He raised his voice a little, which he regretted the minute he'd done it. He had no one to blame but his own pussy self for being such a spineless coward.

His mother's face fell. The look in her eyes was as if she was watching her child make a terrible mistake, unable to stop it from happening. "I'm so sorry, Donovan. You know what your father was like. I was powerless to dissuade him from anything. I did love him, but there were aspects that were hard to swallow. He wanted things his way, and I learned early on if I wanted to avoid his hot temper, I best keep my mouth shut. I know now that was to my detriment. And that of my children, much to my sorrow." She bit her lip. "It took a lot of therapy to get me here."

Donovan's eyes bugged open. "You went to therapy?"

"You bet your bottom dollar I did," she said. "I had to work through a lot of things. Your father was kind of my boss all those years. Again, I did love him. But I resented him too. And I resented what he did to you and Sarah. It wasn't fair of him to dominate everyone the way he did. I know deep down he meant well, and he was operating with the tools he had, which weren't great ones. He came from two parents who were heartless taskmasters, so how could he have done much better?"

Donovan heaved a sigh. "I came from one pain-in-the-ass taskmaster, so is that to be my excuse?"

She clasped his hands in hers. "No, sweetie. Yours is to fix it. Your job is to figure out how to make the amends he was unable to do. You're young—you have your whole life ahead of you. You're a bright man. You survived medical school. Surely you can figure out how to mitigate the damage done by your well-meaning yet kind-of-shitty father."

She smiled and he burst into laughter that filled the room. "Mom! Why, I never!"

She started to laugh and shook her head. "My God, he could be a real pisser, couldn't he, sweetie?"

"You mean the way he would make me take pretest after pretest before any exam I had?"

"And the way he would berate you if you didn't at least get several hits during your baseball games."

"Or the way he belittled me for taking up surfing."

His mother held up her hand in a stop sign signal. "Oh Lord, do not get me started. If I heard it once, I heard it a thousand times: what kind of son are we raising if he has to be on a surfboard with all those lazy boys hanging out at the beach?"

"Dad was a real dick."

She started to laugh. "That's one way to look at it. Like my therapist always tells me, he didn't have the tools to deal with things."

"Tools my ass. He was an asshole." Donovan stood up and leaned over to hug his mother. "I'm glad you outlasted him so you could enjoy your life, Mom."

She nodded, her eyes wistful. "To be honest, me too,

baby. Me too."

Chapter Eight

MADDIE had managed the Salty Scupper, Tamara's bed-and-breakfast on the beach for several years. It wasn't mentally challenging work, but it gave her an opportunity to putz around in the kitchen making sweet treats for the guests and satisfied her need to bake. She'd gotten into baking after her mother left; it was something positive during an otherwise rather grim time of life.

Carter tried to fill the void, but he was still a kid and couldn't ever be her mother anyhow. Or her father. He tried his hardest, though. He'd take her bowling and to the movies and to birthday parties (making sure she had a gift). Sometimes she thought he did so much to keep her busy and occupy her mind that maybe he needed to get away as badly as she did. God, he even told her about sex and her period and tampons and everything, which was pretty darned mortifying to learn from your brother. Yet also comforting. She knew at least Carter was there for her, and that mattered a ton.

Maddie had attended a local community college and took some classes related to cooking while there, yet it wasn't the same. All of her friends had gone away to college, but there wasn't money in her household for that. Carter had saved enough to make sure she could at least attend the community college and finalize her business degree at a smaller branch campus of the state university. But truly, business bored the crap out of her, and in all those years, she had built up a real burning desire to go to pastry school—in Paris! Where she could use her high school French!—and she was so close to having saved enough money to do it. She'd worked hard over the past few years and saved her vacation time and every penny (well, she did squander money on wine, because, well, wine). The tipping point was going to be winning this statewide contest. She knew she could win, but she had to keep her eyes on the prize.

When she got to work, she went through checking out pricing of comparable inns in the area to be sure their rates were competitive during high season. She fielded emails from a night manager who was sick, urging him to find a replacement (the last thing she wanted was to have to trudge in here to work overnight tonight). She helped bus the breakfast dishes and checked out departing customers and the next thing she knew it, it was lunchtime.

This temperate summer weather made her yearn for the childhood days of freedom when you had not a care in the world (that stopped when she was eight, but until then), hang out on the beach and eat Popsicles, play after hours in the lifeguard stand, and not come home till dark. She looked at her watch. She had a good hour or so to hang out near the water's edge and enjoy the quiet of the waves lapping along the shoreline, listening to the caw of the gulls.

She texted Olivia to see if she'd meet her there. Her friend didn't have to work till dinnertime since she was a hostess at Red Fish Blue Fish, the restaurant where Carter worked.

"Dude, I am on my way. I'll bring a chair, and I'll meet you at the inn in twenty minutes."

This would be good. Maddie needed distractions because she was still mentally freeze-framed in the basement of Peg Leg, dry humping her miserable yet gorgeous ex-boyfriend, and loving every last minute of it. She wondered if she needed to seek some psychological counseling to help her resist the urges to capitulate the next time some super-hot, sexy guy employed pheromones or whatever it was that Donovan did to lure her to the dark side.

Was that what happened? Or was she incredibly horny? Or did she have feelings for that SOB after all this time? That seemed downright impossible. How could she? She'd hated him for years. Years! She put so many pins in that stupid voodoo doll of his eventually the stuffing leaked out. And in time, she got tired of bothering with it. Same as she had with her mother. She was not in the mood to scrape all of this up again. Hadn't she grown up and gotten over it? Maybe the fact that she wrapped herself around him like Saran Wrap was a sign that she had. Or perhaps it meant she hadn't gotten off in a while.

She had put out cheese and crackers for the guests to enjoy and started to round up the remnants from their snack time. Before she knew it, it would be time for wine and cheese, but before then, a little jaunt to the ocean's edge seemed precisely what the doctor ordered.

Chapter Nine

"DID Mom make you call me?" Donovan's sister Sarah said as they loaded up her beach stroller—the one with the power blow-up wheels that could four-wheel drive them across a veritable tundra.

"No, she didn't. It was a gentle suggestion. And I took it to heart." Donovan was helping her unload enough shit to go to the damned moon. "Are you sure you're only taking two kids to the beach and not an entire species?"

"Oh, you laugh, brother dearest," she said. "But you wait. Someday you'll be in my shoes and you won't be nearly as tough as I am. Women are tough with this stuff. You'll be like those guys with that zombie-deadened look in your eyes as you pile up your stroller for a day at the beach as if you're planning for Armageddon, and the look in your eyes merely says, 'I just wanted to fuck her,' meaning you had no intention of being trapped in this web of parenthood. You only wanted to get your rocks off."

"Thanks for the vote of confidence, Sar."

"Calling it as I see it. Either that or you'll be like Ryan, who's out golfing while I schlep the kids to the beach."

"He's figured out how to play you. You should demand that he accompany you."

"Dude, I grew up with a man making demands of me. The last thing I would impose on someone else is that shit."

He shrugged. "True dat. Okay, so let's plan a joyful day at the beach. If you help me unfasten these two little monsters from these contraptions in the back seat of the car—"

She shook her head. "You have so much to learn." She reached in and popped the release on one seat belt and led four-year-old Logan to her brother, then grabbed two-year-old Amanda and slung her over her hip, then secured her in the power stroller.

"Logan, hold your uncle's hand in the parking lot," she said as she pushed the stroller down the boardwalk toward the beach.

Donovan had optimistically brought along a book to read and a chair to sink into the soft sand along the water's edge, but he had a sneaking suspicion that was all for naught.

"So, how's this spot look right here?" She pointed to an area with lots of small children and parents.

"Can we go somewhere a bit more private?"

"There is no such thing as private at the beach." She shook her head. "We are all family here. Everyone is looking out for one another's kids, primarily because all the kids are playing together. We are a band of brothers—and sisters—bonded together by the universal need to not lose our children to the ocean or parking lot and hoping some other parent will help you with your child so you can have five minutes' peace. Which, by the way, never happens. Until you're dead."

Her brother cocked his eyebrow as he spread out the large blanket she'd brought along. "Christ, you make parenthood sound so tempting. Like catching some communicable disease that will render you a lesser human being if caught."

"My sweet baby brother, I don't want to discourage you from ever pursuing procreation. I do want you to know it is a heavy-duty duty, one not to be taken lightly. You will not be that dad who is never around—I'll kill you if you are. You will be that dad who is there every step of the way with your wife, helping to ease her burden whenever possible. Because you will want to go home and make sweet love to her that night, and I can assure you she is far more likely to accede to your wishes if you accede to hers. Help her with the kids, she'll help you with your needs. It's a mutually agreeable situation. Capiche?"

Donovan stared at her and blinked three times. "But I just wanted to fuck her." He broke into a broad smile as his sister whacked him with her diaper bag.

In record time, Logan proceeded to traipse sand across the blanket Donovan had laid out. They spread out their remaining stockpile of supplies, first a little pop-up tent contraption that looked to be an ingenious invention. There was the obligatory porta-crib (essential to trap Amanda, who could get from the boardwalk to the ocean's edge in two blinks, according to her mother).

"Gee, sis, maybe you should get a harness and attach one to each kid. Would simplify your life enormously."

She gave him one of those deadpan looks. "You ever hear a small kid scream?"

"Right. So what can I do to help?"

"Glad you asked. We're going to employ the man-on-man defense here, so I'm assigning Logan to you, I'll take care of the safety and livelihood of Amanda. I know Logan was looking forward to building a sandcastle with his beloved Uncle Donovan, so feel free to dig in the beach bag for all the supplies. But first"—she held up her hand, then pulled out a bottle—"sunscreen. You get him, I'll get her." She proceeded to squirt the lotion into her brother's palm, and he started rubbing it into his nephew's skin.

"It is quite the production to plan a relaxing day at the beach, isn't it? I hate to think of what an entire vacation would look like."

"There is no such thing as vacation with small children. It's more of the same at a different venue. Maybe added work given the place isn't childproofed."

"Honey, you are a walking, talking advertisement for condoms." He smiled at her.

"Tell me about it," she said, unscrewing the cap to her water bottle and taking a big swig. "Last time I looked, I was on a date with Ryan, and we were making out behind the lighthouse after the park had closed, and bam, next thing you know, this."

"I'd say a few things happened in the intervening years."

"Yeah, well, you were nowhere near in that time so how would you know?"

He shrugged. "I guess it was a combination of doing what Dad told me I had to do and then wanting to stay as far away from him as possible so he couldn't tell me anything else I had to do. Passive defiance maybe?"

"I hate that Daddy drove you away from us."

"Yeah, well, Dad, plus school, plus a lot of years of training. Then Africa."

"So how was it?"

He shook his head. "So much harder than I thought it would be. Brutal, really. It was exhausting, and everything required so much effort. I mean nothing is like it is here. You have to work ten times as hard to have the basic necessities there. And to get to them requires an act of God—trekking through thigh-deep muds during the rainy season to get somewhere where there's an outbreak of disease. And of course there's no clean water, diseases are rife, peoples' health is often so compromised that it's hard to get them healthy enough to heal. But my God, the people are resilient. And so cheerful and kind. I don't know if I'll ever find such amazing people again."

"Will you go back?"

He shook his head. "Honestly? I think I went there because I was suffering from some sort of life crisis. I needed to go somewhere to give me a chance to reevaluate my choices. The great thing about going somewhere like that is it puts life in great perspective. And it motivated me to want to come back and fix whatever I might have mucked up in my own life before it's too late. So right now, I'm in no hurry for a command performance there. Never say never but not so likely."

"Logan, sweetie, come here and I'll give you your sandwich." She patted a spot next to her on the blanket. "Amanda—you want your peanut butter and jelly?"

The toddler nodded agreeably and reached out to grab the food.

Logan dropped his in the sand but picked it right back up and continued to eat it. Donovan winced.

"So what is it that you've so messed up that you have to fix? I mean, looking from here I see a hardworking man who met his goals and became a doctor and gave back to the community by foregoing the comforts of civilization to work in some of the harshest of conditions. You don't seem like a screwup to me." She winked at him as she took a bite of her sandwich.

He held up his hands. "The one thing I've always regretted terribly, and I didn't realize how much until recently, was how I left things with Maddie." He reached into the soft cooler and pulled out a sandwich for himself. "Awww, you made me ham and cheese. What a thoughtful sister you are."

She shrugged. "What can I say? I aim to please." She grabbed a ponytail holder from her wrist and used it to secure her long, auburn hair. She pulled her daughter into her lap then leaned toward Donovan. "Maddie Henderson, eh?"

He nodded. "You got an opinion on this?"

She closed her eyes. "It's hard for me to say. I was older than you, so I wasn't in the thick of things at home. But I do remember she was a sweet girl. And then you dumped her. I never knew why but figured it wasn't my business."

"Plus you were busy making out with Ryan behind the lighthouse."

She wiped a crumb from her lips. "There was that."

"So am I crazy ten years later hoping I can court her?"

"You might want to change up your verbs. I don't

think that word has been used in such a way since the Civil War."

"Fine. Woo."

"That sounds equally weird." She waved her hand. "Never mind. Makes no difference. So should you try to make amends?"

"That's pretty much what I'm wondering. It's only that I've had this feeling something has been missing in my life. And that seems to be what I keep going back to. I left her so abruptly—"

"Total dick move."

He shook his head. "Tell me about it. I'd sucked down too much of that purple Kool-Aid Dad forced on me."

"He was a persuasive man."

"And not in a good way," Donovan said.

She shook her head. "No. Not so much." She grabbed two juice boxes, slipped the straws out of their cellophane sleeves, and poked one in each box before handing them to the kids. "Sorry, gang, Mom forgot you needed liquid to wash those sandwiches down."

"How do you focus?"

She laughed. "Moms are masters at multitasking." She grabbed a bag of Goldfish from the cooler and gave each kid a handful of them. "So do you have a plan of attack?"

Donovan shook his head. "Well…"

"That was a loaded word."

He huffed out a breath. "Oooh, yeah." He grabbed the bag of Goldfish and poured some into his palm. "You know how she and I were trivia freaks? Well, I found out she's still into it and was going to be at a trivia night at the Peg Leg, so I went there."

"Oh, I'm sure she appreciated you dropping the boom like that."

He shook his head. "Not so much. But."

She held up her finger. "Ahhh, the old 'but' qualifier. Spill!"

"This is super weird telling my sister this."

She waved her hand. "Oh, please. I pushed two watermelons out of my vagina. I can deal with some dirty details."

He burst out laughing. "You should consider working the nightclub circuit with your shtick." He took a deep breath. "At intermission, she bolted downstairs and looked upset, so I ran after her. We ended up alone downstairs and then she started crying and talking about how she had gotten over me and now here I was and the next thing you know we're going at it hot and heavy in the murky, dimly lit basement of the Peg Leg."

"How romantic."

"Believe it or not it was kind of romantic. I mean it would have been better at the Four Seasons, but beggars can't be choosers."

"So then what's the problem? You had reunion sex—"

"If you're keeping score, we didn't go all the way."

"Ah, so she left you high and dry."

He shook his head. "The game was starting up—her team came in search of her."

"Awkward."

"Tell me about it."

"So lemme guess. She freaked out. Regretted what she did. Stormed off in a huff, and you're left scratching your head wondering what you did wrong."

"It's as if you're a woman or something."

"I hope you're not implying that women do stupid things like that."

"I am indeed."

"Well, then I'll imply you did an even stupider thing in the first place."

"And I'll concur with you wholeheartedly."

"So now you know she's still got some long-buried hots for you. But you have to break through the emotional shield she rightly built up to protect herself from the likes of you."

He tapped his skull with his finger. "Brilliant deduction, dear Watson."

"Well it's simple enough," she said.

Just then Amanda said she had to go potty. And Logan asked his uncle if he'd build a sandcastle. So much for the sage advice from his wise older sister. Advice-us interruptus from the spawn.

So he collected the pile of sandcastle equipment and grabbed for his nephew's hand and walked down closer to the edge of the water, past where the ocean stopped encroaching, and the two sat down on the hard-packed sand.

"You think you might be a builder someday, Logan?" he said with a grin.

"I want to be a fireman."

Donovan nodded. "Well, knowing how these structures are built will help you with that job too." The two of them started digging and filling the molds with sand, then packing them into place. "You want a big moat, like this." He used a nearby shell to scoop out a bunch of sand.

"For all the crocodiles?"

"You bet. And snakes. You'll want poisonous snakes in there too. Maybe a hippo or two. They're pretty aggressive."

"And a lion. No one will come near my castle with a lion guarding it."

Donovan scruffed his nephew's hair, and they smiled at one another as Donovan looked up and saw a pair of emerald-green eyes flashing at him. Maddie. With her hair blowing freely in the wind, the air catching her sundress and blowing it upward. She looked so free and natural, it made his heart ache.

Then he felt something tugging on the hair on his chest. "Ow!" he said, looking down to see Logan trying to get his attention.

"Uncle Donovan! Uncle Donovan!" the boy said. "Who's that?"

Donovan looked at the boy, then at Maddie and grinned. "That, my boy, is the future Mrs. Donovan Reeves."

Chapter Ten

"SO are you ready to fess up about you and that guy from last night?" Olivia slung her backpack over her shoulder as they took the steps along the little boardwalk that bisected the dunes down to the beach.

Maddie stopped to look at her redheaded friend with the super pale complexion.

"Don't you need to put some sunscreen on or something?"

Olivia gave Maddie's shoulder a friendly push. "You think you can distract me, but you can't. Believe me, I saw the looks you two exchanged last night. And behind that searing anger were the banked coals of smoldering heat. Downright incendiary. And it did not escape my notice that you disappeared for an awfully long time last night. And the only two people who hadn't returned to the game after intermission were you and him."

Maddie pointed toward the sky. "Is that a hawk up there?"

Olivia looked up and then threw her friend the side-eye. "You know that I am relentless, right? Like that time you went on a blind date with the guy I fixed you up with, and you wouldn't tell me anything about the date?"

"You were such a pain in my ass."

"Right? Didn't I pinch you till I got it out of you?"

"Yes. That hurt, too!"

"Well, it was good to know that he had bad breath. My reputation was on the line. I wouldn't want to send a bad-breathed man out on another date, what with the chance he might make someone puke."

Maddie laughed. "Cadaver breath. That's what it was. I never did thank you enough for that shitty date."

"I'm sorry for foisting him on you—he was a friendly guy, though. But I'm also grateful I've reminded you about my powers of persuasion." She started making pincer movements with her fingertips and reaching toward her friend.

"Get away from me!" Maddie swatted at her and started flicking at her pinching fingertips until the two of them were laughing so hard Maddie almost fell backward onto the sand.

"Honestly you are such a pain in my butt," Maddie said, taking a bite of her chicken salad sandwich. "I wanted to come down to the ocean and clear my head, and instead, you're going to nag me the whole time?"

"Consider it free therapy."

"Oh, so you're a trained expert on the emotional lives of others?"

"No, but I'm a girl. And I'm intuitive. And I can be objective since I'm someone you've never talked to about this boy. And he is cute. And has something for you, based on how his stare practically burned its way through your body."

Maddie blushed. "That's not true."

"I'm telling you. Every time you weren't looking at him, he was looking at you. I was worried he was going to strip you naked and have his way with you right on the bar."

Maddie smacked at her friend. "Stop. You're embarrassing me!"

"And I'm going to keep embarrassing you until you tell me what the hell was going on with you two."

Maddie heaved a big sigh. "It's boring. And super old stuff."

"I love boring stories."

Maddie shook her head. "Fine. He and I dated in high school. We were pretty serious for a long time. He was two years older than I was and was going away to college. I saw him like a day before he left for college and thought we'd have a formal goodbye before he drove away, but then he disappeared. No goodbye, no 'I love you,' no 'miss you,' nothing. Didn't answer phone calls or texts or anything. His jerk father finally answered my call and told me to do Donovan a favor and let him go. End of story."

Olivia crossed her hands over her heart. "Donovan… What a dreamy name."

"He basically ghosted me, Olivia. Just because his name is good doesn't mean he's not a complete jerk."

"So how long ago was this?"

Maddie took a bite of her sandwich, then frowned. "Ten or so years."

"So, like, a third of your life ago?"

"What's your point?"

"That it seems an awfully long time ago to carry a grudge. Even if he was the biggest dick on the planet, which it sounds like he was at least vying for. And so maybe in ten years the boy has become a man and recognized the error of his ways. Maybe it's worth giving him another shot."

"Spoken like a true unscarred woman."

As they reached the ocean's edge, Olivia stopped and stood, staring at Maddie. "Dude. You think I haven't been screwed over by plenty of guys over the years? Try this: I dated a guy for three years, and that whole time I wouldn't have sex with him. I was still hung up on the stupid idea of saving myself for marriage. And ultimately I saw the light and decided the time was right to sleep with him, and we did, and I never heard back from him again. Like gone. Like that." She snapped her fingers.

"What is this with guys and the fuck-and-run thing?" Maddie said.

"I think it's because guys can be super soulless." They both laughed. "But seriously, I don't know. Maybe it has to do with their ability to compartmentalize. Maybe some of them are complete chickenshits. Maybe they have no ability to grasp things on an emotional level. Or maybe they chose to be assholes at that place and time."

"D—all of the above," Maddie said.

"So did I hold a grudge against James forever?"

Maddie rolled her eyes. "Knowing you, you invited him to your place for dinner and told him not to worry about it."

"Hell no. I called and texted and bugged the shit out of him for weeks. Then I literally put a paper bag with dog poop in it on his doorstep, set it on fire, then rang the doorbell and ran."

"You did not."

"Of course I did. He deserved at least that."

"Have you ever seen him since?"

She shook her head. "He threatened to get a restraining order against me or something like that. I decided he wasn't worth going to jail for."

"Duh."

"But I also reconciled myself with the truth: he wasn't right for me. I don't know what his deal was. Maybe he felt guilty after I finally slept with him? For all I know he'd been sleeping with other women too and decided they were better. But to hell with him. I had to focus on me and what was best for me and I put him out of my head for good."

"Which is what I did with Donovan. I mean it was hard. I was crestfallen. He was the first person I shared my heart with after my mom left. It had taken me a long time to get there. And I trusted him with all my heart. So it was no easy feat to erase him from my life. But I eventually did. I moved on. But then this."

Olivia splashed her feet in the water. "So what happened last night?"

Maddie dug her toes in the wet sand and let her feet sink deeper into it. "I mean I was so taken aback by his showing up. He's been gone for so many years. And there he was. Oh, and I know you tease me about being a little bit obsessive with this whole trivia thing, but I guess that was a leftover from our time together—it was something we shared." She tucked her hair behind her ear. "Well, you know how much this state championship means to me. It's a big deal. And who shows up but someone who messed my whole mind up—I couldn't even focus. But then the worst thing was he and I had this thing together—"

"Thing?"

Maddie shook her head. "This is kind of weird and you're going to laugh at me. You have to swear to me you'll never repeat this to a soul. And you also have to promise you'll never mock me about this."

Olivia traced her fingers in an X across her heart. "Cross my heart."

"So trivia was kind of like foreplay with Donovan and me. I don't know why, but I think maybe it was that he was so damned smart, and it turned me on to see how his mind worked. And somehow that ended up parlaying into how the two of us would end up going at it hot and heavy each time we challenged each other to harder and harder questions."

"Okay, that is weird, but who am I to judge?"

Maddie smacked her arm. "So last night it was this freakish déjà vu thing, and as his team answered questions correctly, I knew he was the one coming up with most of the answers. And it resurrected all those feelings and emotions in a giant ball of angst. When we had a break, I ran down to the bathroom to collect myself."

"Only he was there to collect you instead?"

"I came out of the bathroom and he was standing in the shadows. And I started to cry. And he pulled me against his chest to comfort me. And I don't know what came over me, but somehow all of a sudden *I* started making out with *him*, of all things."

Olivia clapped her hands. "Squee! This is so excellent! All on your terms. So you were the initiator. As it should be."

"I think it was more like I was the desperately horny idiot who should have held her ground but instead went at it with the guy like a bobcat in heat."

"What happens with bobcats in heat?"

"You don't want to know. It's gruesome."

"I'll take your word for it." She pressed on. "So what happened next? Did you do it? In the basement of the Peg Leg? I'm sure you won't have been the first. Inquiring minds want to know."

"We didn't do *it*, per se. But pretty darned close."

"Who won—you or him?"

"I didn't know it was a win-or-lose proposition."

"Did you get him off?"

"I can't believe you're asking me that."

"I'm hoping not. I'm hoping it was one-sided. It's the least he could do after all this time. Rub one out for you."

Maddie put her hands over her face. "You didn't actually say that, did you?"

"Of course I did. This is the twenty-first century. You need to claim your seat at the sexual table, my friend."

Maddie rolled her eyes. "Well, I sure did that last night."

"Brava. Exactly what you needed. So are you dating now?"

"Are you crazy? That was a one-off. I can't go back to him after all that." She took a sip of her bottle of water.

"But that was a lifetime ago, Mads. Maybe it's time to let go of the anger and get some more of that hand action."

Maddie spat out the water she'd sipped. "I think it's best if I let the past be the past. I don't need to rehash everything and oy, it's more than I think I want to deal with."

"C'mon, Mads. Give peace a chance."

"I feel like I should hold my lighter aloft."

"See where the whole thing takes you. Did he move back here? Or is he here on a visit? Is he trying to make amends with you? Does he want to pick up where you left off?"

"I have no idea. We didn't exactly talk. At least not with words."

"Oh yeah, his hands did all the talking, did they?"

"You are so nosy."

"I'm getting my vicarious thrills, thank you." Olivia reached into her backpack and pulled out a box of Girl Scout Thin Mints, opened a sleeve, and offered some to her friend.

"Who takes Girl Scout cookies to the beach?" Maddie said. "Besides, aren't these stale by now?"

"Nah. These things never go stale. You could come back after the Apocalypse and survive on Girl Scout cookies—they're that perfect."

Maddie popped one into her mouth. "So? Satisfied now?"

"Hell no. I want to hear the rest of the story. I can't wait to hear if there's a happily ever after involved with it. Maybe he got hit in the head with a coconut and forgot everything from the past. But then lo and behold he runs into you and it rekindles all the emotions he thought he'd lost, all returning to the surface, helping to heal his wounds."

"Yeah, you've been watching too many Disney movies. But I've gotta get back to work."

"We're not done yet, though. Look." She pulled out her phone and sent a text message.

"What was that?"

"I texted Tamara and told her you were running late, that you had an emergency."

"You did not do that."

"Yes, I did! It's a beautiful day, and we haven't finished this deep discussion. I won't be happy till you tell me you're going to go for it with Donovan." Her phone dinged and she looked down, then gave Maddie a thumbs-up. "Tamara said take all the time you want. She's got things under control."

Maddie held her hands up. "I have no freaking idea what I'm going to do, okay? But I have to get back to work, even if you did write me a school excuse."

She turned to head back toward the bed-and-breakfast, only to see Donovan not ten feet from her, shirtless, his bare chest strong and beautiful, with enough chest hair to make her swoon with desire.

"Shoot me now," she said to her friend as her eyes met his in time for her to hear him speak.

"Uncle Donovan! Uncle Donovan!" the kid next to him said. "Who's that?"

Donovan looked at the boy, then at Maddie and grinned. "That, my boy, is the future Mrs. Donovan Reeves."

Chapter Eleven

MADDIE froze in her tracks.

What did he say? *The future Mrs. Donovan Reeves?* In what alternate universe?

She turned and fixed her gaze on his.

"I'm sorry, but what did you say?"

Donovan's face was already tanned, but she could see the blush creep up his neck for having been caught.

"I was telling my nephew Logan, here, who you were.

"Sarah has a kid now?"

"Actually two. The other one is Amanda."

"I guess the whole world moved on." She paused, crossed her arms, and glared at him. "Look, Donovan. Please don't pee on my leg and then tell me it's raining, 'kay? You of all people should know I'm not stupid."

No sooner did she say the words than she realized her language was a bit rough to say in front of a little kid. Oops.

"Uncle Donovan—did you go pee on her leg? Mom gets mad if I even pee on the floor next to the toilet."

Donovan cracked one of those smiles—the ones she found so damn irresistible, with the dimples all innocent-like. "No, Bud. That would be gross. It was only an expression."

"Someone say something about people peeing on legs?"

Maddie looked over to see Donovan's sister Sarah holding the tiny hand of a mini-her.

"Oh, hi! Maddie Henderson! What a nice surprise to see you here! I'd like you to meet my kids, Amanda and Logan."

Maddie squatted down to get to their level and gave them a wave. "Hey, you two. I'm Maddie. So great to meet you."

The kids mumbled something indecipherable, which was fine. She wasn't here to win the hearts and minds of toddlers and preschoolers; she was here to chill on her lunch hour.

Maddie looked around to find where Olivia had disappeared to, and curse her if she hadn't somehow evaporated tout de suite. What was it with everyone abandoning her in her time of need?

Cue Donovan's sister, ready to pull her own little disappearing act.

"Hey, buddy," she said, leaning down to her son. "What say you, me, and Amanda take a little walk down the beach to look for dead crabs."

"My favorite!" Logan said. And then Amanda toddled after him, clearly loving whatever her big brother loved.

"I'll be back in a little bit, Donovan. Don't do anything I wouldn't do."

He rolled his eyes. "Big sisters," he said to Maddie. "Can't live with 'em, can't push 'em overboard."

Maddie suddenly found herself speechless, staring at

the shirtless Donovan in his too-sexy board shorts. His chest had just enough hair to make her mouth water. That is if it could water, but instead, it was dry as a bone. Her tongue felt like it adhered to the roof of her mouth as if she'd licked one too many envelopes. Having licked his mouth only hours earlier, the thought of it had parched her mouth.

Maddie toed the sand at her feet.

"Can I invite you to my lair?" Donovan said, pointing toward the turf he and Sarah had staked earlier. "Of course the tent isn't big enough for the two of us. Or even one of us. But there's a blanket there, albeit covered with sand. And a porta-crib in case you get tired."

Maddie stuck out her lower lip. "I guess I can sit for a few minutes before I have to get back to work."

"You work nearby? A lifeguard, maybe?"

She rolled her eyes. "If lifeguards have to wear business attire." She pointed toward the B and B. "I manage that bed-and-breakfast. Nothing too exciting, but it works."

"Ahhh, in the travel industry, eh?" he patted the blanket next to him, offering up a seat.

"I'd hardly call it travel. Except that I deal with others who are traveling." She sat down on the edge of the blanket and crossed her legs. She began to play with sand in her hand—anything to distract her from this awkward situation. "What about you? Heard you'd become a big doctor."

He shrugged. "I don't know about big. I am a medical doctor, for what it's worth."

"So your dad got his wish."

Donovan frowned. "My father had a habit of doing

that."

"So you did it for him, or for you?"

He shook his head. "A little bit of both, maybe."

"So where do you practice?"

"I'd been up in Boston, but I was feeling antsy and took off for a while. Went to work for an NGO and lived in Africa."

"So much to unpack in that sentence. So you went to medical school in Boston?"

"Nope. New York. Residency in Boston and I stayed on for a little while after."

"And Africa because?"

Donovan turned and lay down on his side, facing Maddie, bending his knee, and propping up one leg. Her eyes were inextricably drawn to that trail of hair that led from his taut navel to below the edge of his suit. She thought her head might spin off her shoulders at the sight. The world could be a cruel, cruel place, taunting her as it was.

"I had this constant sense of unfinished business. Like something was missing. I don't know. I couldn't quite put my finger on it. But I wanted—I needed—change. And radical change, at that. So I applied to work for Médicins Sans Frontières, known as MSF. Next thing I knew I was on a plane to Kinshasa, in the DRC in Central Africa."

"Wow. You're much braver than I."

"Not a matter of bravery. More like I had to pursue a mandate."

She let out a laugh tinged with bitterness. "You were always good at following mandates."

He frowned. "I was indeed. It's my shame I've had

to live with for a very long time."

"So now that you've returned from Africa, what are you doing? I'm assuming you're not here to stay." One tiny part of her hoped she was wrong, entertaining some foolish reunion fantasy. She knew it was idiotic, but it was hard to tamp down the glimmers of hope that loved to force their way through an otherwise pragmatic spirit like a weed through a crack in the sidewalk.

He shook his head. "I haven't figured that out. I'm still decompressing from things. The DRC was amazing, but it was intense. I had to learn to live on the edge, which is funny because I thought medical school forced me to do that. But this was that intense times a thousand. We worked in areas without much food, with no potable water—and usually water of any form was miles away. To get basic medical supplies to critical sites required unbelievable amounts of coordination and work." He paused to grab waters out of the cooler for both of them. "And once there—often tiny villages in remote parts of the country on the edge of the jungle—we slept in tents and dealt with mosquitos that could carry malaria or the tsetse fly with sleeping sickness, and heat and humidity and fatigue, and those were the good bits. The bad bits were losing patients when you got there too late. Or holding a mother whose baby had just died in her arms from dehydration after suffering from deadly diarrhea. It wasn't for the faint of heart, and it left me deeply moved."

Maddie had shifted and lay on her side in the same position, facing him. "I know I'm being redundant here, but, well, wow. It sounds remarkable. Makes me feel like a total slacker for doing what I do, which is a big fat not much."

He reached out and tucked a strand of hair behind her ear. "I don't want you to diminish your life because of my experiences. What I've done is no reflection on what you've done. This was my path to get me to where I am right now."

"Which is… messing with the head of the girl you jilted in a bad way a lifetime ago?"

He frowned, then ran his fingers through his hair. "Dish it out, Mads. I deserve everything you want to say to me."

She squinted at him. "I'm not sure this is the time or place for this conversation." She glanced at her phone to check the time. "I mean I've got to get back to work, or I'm going to have to find a new path to figure out what the hell I'm doing in my life. But I do have to ask you: was I just some hideous sea hag that you had to shake off like a clump of wet seaweed that clings to your head after a wave tackles you hard? If so, I don't understand why you wasted so much time with me only to do what you did."

Donovan held her gaze, not answering at all. Then he shifted himself closer to her, reaching his arms out and pulling her into his embrace. He pressed her head toward his shoulder with one hand—one large, warm hand—the very hand that probably performed surgery in the jungle and saved babies from death and held others as they released their final breath. How could she hate a man who had hands like that?

"You have to realize that this wasn't at all about you, Maddie. It was all about me and my shortcomings. My inability to stand up to my father. It was about my being a coward and not having the courage to do the right thing because I didn't know how to do it without hurting you. And so I hurt you even more by slinking away."

His chest expanded and contracted as he spoke and started to sob, and that was so not something Maddie had anticipated. Was he crying over her? Over what he'd destroyed? Or was it something more significant? Crying about what a prick his father was? She could vouch for that; he was indeed a prick. One time he'd made Donovan stand at attention for two straight hours when he failed to mow the lawn. Or was he crying about those babies dying in their mothers' arms while he was helpless to save them?

It was all too much for her to deal with. On some level, she knew this was her cue to provide solace to him—that maybe all along Donovan had needed some comfort and assurance that no one had given him. It made her sad. But more than anything, it scared her. This all flew in the face of the Teutonic-strength emotional wall she'd constructed around herself to save her from having to deal with messy emotions. She needed to step back and get a grip, or she'd fall right back in love with Donovan Reeves, and that was so not going to happen. No way, no how.

She pressed her hands against his chest—oh God, that chest. She wanted to keep them there, soaking in the warmth of his body, her fingers twining through his chest hair and maybe finding their way lower on his torso, right down to the trail that transfixed her. She could slide them beneath the edge of his waistband and make her way to his hard cock, wrapping her fingers around its velvet length and stroking gently. And maybe she could get a groan from him when she first placed her fingers on it, and that would warm her right in the pit of her stomach, only not truly in the pit of her stomach. More like right in the part of her body where she knew his cock would fit so perfectly. And it was tempting—oh so tempting. But no—what a mistake that would be. The flood of memories washed over her and that was something she was unprepared to deal with.

She pushed a little harder and slipped her head from around his hand and sat up, straightening her sundress as she did so.

"Um, I need to get back to work." She got up and stood in front of him. From there she could see the bulge in his shorts, along with the reflection of hidden tears in his eyes. She was being a real jerk, and she knew it. But she had to be. She couldn't go there with Donovan again. It would be too risky and her heart couldn't take it. She gave him a superficial wave. "Good luck with everything. Let me know next time you're in town."

With that, she turned and walked away, feeling like a coward but not knowing what it would take for her to be brave instead.

Chapter Twelve

WELL, that went well. Not.

Donovan peered around to the collection of families with small children in the immediate vicinity—he was parked in the Kiddyland of beach spots—and he cringed. God, who here had heard this conversation? Did someone hear him sob—actually sob? What the fuck? Where did that shit come from? One thing Donovan did not do was sob.

Well, actually that was a lie. There was many a time when he was in Africa that he cried. Like the time he held the hand of a young mother as she lay dying of AIDS and begged him to care for her three small children. They didn't even speak the same language, but he knew what she wanted. And he told her he'd do his best to help them. Which he did. He got them together with a social worker who was going to try to find family to help. But he had to be realistic—this was not the place to be left orphaned. Life was hard enough here with parents watching out for you. On your own? It would be grim.

He cried many times. Once when they took a day off and trekked in the Rwenzori Mountains in search of the famed gorillas, he cried when they came upon a family of gorillas and watched a new mother nursing her baby. He cried upon learning that soldiers regularly shot and killed these magnificent creatures or lopped off their hands for souvenirs. If the world was a hard place, these dark parts of Africa were even tougher. And it seemed that, yeah, the harder it got, maybe the more it got to him. Or maybe he needed it to get to him. Maybe he spent too many years hardened up against pain, and the hurt needed to leak out, one way or another. After all, it wasn't doing him a whole lot of good built up inside him like some emotional jelly doughnut that's for damn sure.

He rolled onto his stomach and closed his eyes, giving his cock a chance to deflate, yet again, while he stayed there with his thoughts. Any minute, Sarah would be back and he'd have to put on a happy face for them. The bummer was the person most likely to give him a reason to smile—to smile and mean it—was the person who'd given him the biggest brush-off of his life.

"So?"

Donovan could hear his sister's voice, and he lifted his head. He must've drifted off to sleep for fifteen minutes. At least now he could stand up without anyone seeing what Maddie Henderson had done to him before she took off in haste.

He shook his head.

"Awww, sweetie, I'm sorry," she said. "Anything I can do to help out?"

He chuckled. "The quick ditch with the kids was about as much as you could, and that wasn't enough, unfortunately."

She wrinkled her nose. "Maybe she's scared."

"Of what?"

She threw him the side-eye. "Of being hurt, dummy. You gotta admit—you hurt her badly last time. It's not easy to trust after that kind of thing."

He let out a sigh. "You're right. But maybe she'll never trust me again and there's nothing I can do about it."

"You gotta keep pressing away. Sooner or later you'll know. I'd say the fact that she did what she did with you at the Peg Leg shows that deep down she's still interested."

"Yeah, well, she scooted out of here so fast you'd have thought I'd set her pants on fire."

She smirked. "Wasn't that what you did last night?"

He nodded.

"So figure out how to do that again. Chip away at her wall. You'll get there. It might take awhile, but you will."

"Where are you going, Uncle Donovan?" Logan asked.

"Donvun," his sister parroted.

Donovan got up from the blanket and scooped Logan up in one arm and Amanda in his other. "I'm going to swim in the ocean with you two little monsters." He made a roaring sound and ran off down the sand, then splashed into the shallow water to fits of giggles and squeals.

With that, he knew for sure he was home again—the one place where he must confront his demons about why he let go of the best thing that ever happened to him.

It had been a week since he'd seen Maddie. Tonight was trivia night and he wrestled with whether to go. He wanted badly to see her, but he also didn't want to throw a wrench into her plans. He hoped to give her the space but didn't want to let her think he was expendable. It was a fine line he was walking.

"Fuck it," he said, throwing on a pair of low-slung, gray sweatpants and a tight white T-shirt. He brushed his teeth, grabbed his car keys, and backed out of the driveway on his way to the Peg Leg. He couldn't not go.

When he arrived, he saw many of the same teams as last week and the three women who'd teamed up with Maddie for Team Trivia Newton John. Only there was no Maddie to be found.

He'd planned to hang out and not watch, so he went up to the bar and ordered a beer, scouring the room for any sign of Maddie. At last, he couldn't take not knowing and slipped into the empty seat at their table.

"Ladies," he said. "I don't believe we've officially met. I'm Donovan Reeves."

"Well if you're not a sight for sore eyes," the

redheaded woman said as she reached out her hand. "I'm Olivia Singletary—I'm the one who foisted Maddie on you at the beach last week. Ever since then she has been as skittish as a hermit crab. Any idea what's up with her?"

He shook his head. "I wish I could tell you. I imagine I scared her. And I'm sorry for that—especially if this broke up your foursome."

They shook their heads. "We do this for fun," the brunette with short hair said. "So not like this is some do-or-die thing for us. I'm Tamara Thompson, by the way." She waved her hand at him. "It's Maddie who takes this thing seriously. We all know she answers ninety-nine percent of the questions. We're along for the ride—"

"And the beer," said the woman with the dirty blond bob. "Hey—I'm Jesse Montgomery."

"So no Maddie for trivia night?"

"It's downright bizarre. She hasn't answered our calls or texts. We have no idea what is going on with her."

He heaved a sigh. "Well, we have two choices." They all looked at him. "First is I can fill in for her tonight since you guys are left in the lurch. The second is I go find her and figure out what her deal is, so I help make things better for her."

They barely let him finish the sentence before Olivia was writing down Maddie's address on a cocktail napkin for him. "Sweetie, you need to go straighten her out. She's got state championships coming up this weekend. She is counting on winning that money. But no way is she going to do that if she's stuck sulking in her bedroom. Please, go finish whatever it is you've started so she can officially get her shit together, would ya?"

Donovan pursed his lips and nodded. This was going to be a Herculean task. He had no choice but to try even if it meant destroying any chance of a future with her for good.

Chapter Thirteen

THE scene on the beach kept haunting Maddie—how much Donovan was reaching out to her and how much she was incapable of allowing that connection to happen. It was hers to make or break. Or keep broken, more like it. And if she did that, how was she going to feel about it? Could she ever trust him again? There'd be no point in reestablishing anything with him if she couldn't. But what if she was missing out on the greatest opportunity in her life? Not to sound dramatic, but what she'd had with Donovan was pretty amazing while it lasted. Certainly nothing she'd replicated with another man since. Not that she'd tried—she'd pretty much protected herself in emotional Bubble Wrap after that, and it's hard to have a truly visceral relationship with someone when you don't let your guard down to be the true you.

Instead of trying to figure things out, she went to her default setting, emotionally numb, combined with a whole lot of stress eating because, well, ice cream. She was pretty sure God had invented ice cream so heartbroken women could have a Plan B.

The shitty thing was the hurdle she seemed unable to transcend. The way Donovan bailed on her was so reminiscent of what her mother did that she couldn't forgive him for it. Cut and run seemed to shadow her like an overzealous bodyguard, never leaving her sight. And Donovan's disappearance only seemed to intensify her mother's betrayal a hundredfold. How did she ever get past that?

And yet here he was, no longer the apparition that visited her in her dreams, causing her to constantly wonder *what if?* But instead he was here and offering a fig leaf—or was that an olive branch?—and she wasn't able to reach out to accept it. Which made her wonder—was something wrong with her? If someone apologizes and genuinely means it, aren't you supposed to be the big person and accept it with grace? And if you can't, then shame on you, right?

Ugh. She was at wit's end. Even her wise brother Carter couldn't dope slap her into a better place.

She'd gone to Red Fish Blue Fish, the restaurant where he was the head chef. He'd finished plating the last few meals, and removed his chef's jacket and met her at the long copper bar in the front of the restaurant for drinks.

"Geez, Maddie, what's up with you?" He pointed at her eyes, which had dark circles under them.

"Thanks for the warm greetings, brother." She flipped him the finger.

"Just worried for your welfare, but you already know that."

"Yeah, I do. I know you've always cared for me even when no one else did."

"Oh, this doesn't sound good. I haven't heard you sound so self-pitying since—"

"Since Donovan ditched me?"

He tapped on the bar to get the bartender's attention and ordered two Sazeracs.

"You trying to get me drunk?"

He nodded. "Looks like that's what you need. Am I right?"

She curled her lip. "Yeah, sadly, you are."

"So back to the Donovan bit... I was afraid to invoke his name, but since you took the liberty of doing so, yeah. After you finally got over him, I thought you wouldn't fall into that pit of despair again. What's—or should I say who's—got you so glum?"

The bartender placed the drinks in front of them and Carter tipped his glass to hers before taking a swig.

"I'll give you a hint. Rhymes with Monovan."

Her brother squinted his green eyes and scrubbed his blond hair with his hand. "You're going to have to provide more details. I mean it can't be all of a sudden you're mooning over that guy again. He's been gone for a lifetime."

She took a sip of her drink, gasped at the strength of it, then nodded her head slowly. "Gone, but not forgotten. Because here he is back in my life. The ghost of breakups past."

"Donovan Reeves is back in town?"

"Back and being the same old Donovan I knew and loved. Which doesn't help me much."

He threw her the side-eye. "And why not? Isn't that what you wanted all those years ago?"

She glared at him. "Um, yeah. Ten-plus years ago. But now? It's a kick in the gut for him to be back."

"What brought him back here?"

She ran her fingers through her hair. "I don't know.

Life crisis?"

"And part of that life crisis involves you?"

"Evidently so."

"So he's back and trying to make amends, and you're not having any of it?"

Maddie closed her eyes, trying to figure out how to make sense of it.

"Carter, I don't know what I want and don't want. I know I wanted him. Badly. And he didn't want me just as badly. And now he says he wants me just as badly, and it's not that I don't want him—I don't think any amount of hate will ever cancel out how much I wanted him—but I mean, come on. I need to have some self-respect, don't I? What kind of fool would I be if I went there again? At this late date? After I've purged him from my psyche at last?"

Carter frowned and circled his finger along the rim of his glass. "Maybe you'd be the kind of fool who has the capacity to forgive and to love again?"

"That makes me sound cold and heartless if I can't."

He held up his hands. "No offense intended. I wasn't saying that. I mean it's a great gift to be able to let go of anger and pain. It's a gift to you and to the person who hurt you. Maybe this is a test for you to see if you're up to the task?"

"Well, shit, Carter. I didn't ask to have any stupid tasks thrown at me. I'm simply going about my life, minding my business, not looking for trouble, when trouble finds me."

"Maybe It's the kind of trouble you needed in your life."

"Are you suggesting my life is dull and boring?"

"Not at all. I'm saying you've been plugging along with things and it's all fine and good, but I think even you might admit something was missing in your life."

She growled. "Oh, you mean a man? A stupid man?"

He chuckled. "A stupid man is precisely what I meant. I know you've been spending many a sleepless night bemoaning the lack of stupid men in your life." He swatted at her with a cardboard coaster that was next to him.

"You know what I mean."

He shrugged. "I do. But, maybe the universe is talking to you, Mads. And maybe it's demanding that you answer it."

"So you're telling me I need to pick up where we left off and everything will be hunky-dory."

"Did I say that?" He looked at Jake, the bartender. "Did you hear me say that?"

Jake shook his head. "I didn't hear anything. I'm staying out of this."

"What I might suggest, however," Carter added, "was that you do a little bit of soul-searching and figure out what you want, what you're willing to forgive, and what is beyond your capacity to accept."

Maddie downed the rest of her drink, then set her glass on the bar. "You're not going to make my decision for me, are you?"

He shook his head. "Nope. And that's what you were hoping for, wasn't it?"

She nodded. "Kinda sorta."

"Sorry, honey. This is all yours. And there's not a right or wrong answer. But I hope you'll take some time to think it through from all angles before you come to a conclusion."

She rose from the barstool, even more uncertain than ever.

"I guess I'll go home and drown my sorrows in a quart of rocky road. Maybe the marshmallows will tell me what to do, like divining tea leaves."

"I trust you'll manage fine however you do it, Mads." Her brother hugged her. "You fine to drive?"

She nodded. "Yeah. As much as I'd love to get super drunk and make this all go away, I know that won't help matters. I'm going to go on a pouting hiatus and try to figure things out. Talk to you later."

What a difference a week made. Last Wednesday at this time, Maddie was prepping for trivia night with the utmost of confidence. She'd worn her favorite sundress, applied makeup and an extra layer of lipstick. She'd run through her list of life affirmations to prime the pump and make sure she was ready.

This week, instead, she hadn't showered in a day. Hadn't shaved her legs in the better part of a week. Not like anyone else would be in the general vicinity of her gorilla legs, so what did it matter? It was a crapshoot if she'd even brushed her teeth yet for the day. She hoped ice cream and Doritos created some sort of slurry of grit that would wash away the worst of what had built up on her teeth overnight. Getting up to deal with daily ablutions was more than she could bear.

And ultimately, who gave a shit about trivia? It was, after all, quite trivial. Instead of dragging her emotionally compromised ass out of bed and joining her friends at the Peg Leg for the last prep night before the big weekend, she had holed up beneath her comforter in the dark recesses of her apartment binge-watching *The Notebook*. Because, well, watching it once would never be enough. At this point, nothing would ever be enough.

Chapter Fourteen

DONOVAN parked his blue BMW convertible in a space in front of the apartment complex where Maddie lived. The neighborhood was a mix of weathered wood-sided houses and two-story condos surrounded by marsh and the sound, which extended for a good distance on the horizon. Her condo complex was on the sound side of the narrow peninsula that was buffered by ocean on one side, inlet on the other.

He got out of his car and mounted the nearby steps to the second story and walked down the open-air hallway till he got to her unit. He went to knock, then paused and took a deep breath, running his fingers through his hair. This felt like a make-or-break moment, and he didn't want to blow it. So before he knocked, which might yield no response if she was hibernating beneath a pile of blankets in her bedroom, unwilling to answer the door, he decided to try the knob in case it was unlocked.

He wrapped his fingers around the handle and ever so quietly turned the knob as he pushed gingerly, hoping the deadbolt hadn't been closed. Mercifully the door opened. He was going to have to talk with her about safety. No woman should be holed up in her apartment with such ready access to strangers. Meanwhile he figured she might give him a ream of shit for taking the liberty of opening the thing himself. So be it.

He tiptoed into the living room, which was bathed in darkness but for the moon casting its light into the dining room through a long sliding glass door that led to a balcony overlooking the ocean. The walls, the furnishings, the carpet were all white, and there were a few large brightly colored paintings on the walls throughout the place. It made him sad to realize that it was her place and hers alone. That it wasn't a home they shared, which was how things could have been. Instead it reflected what seemed like the starkness of her life.

It also drew attention to the transient life he'd lived for the past decade or so. There wasn't a place he could call home. In his undergraduate years, he lived in a succession of places that were basically someplace to put his head at night, nothing more. In medical school, he was home so rarely he couldn't remember what his apartments were like back then. Same for his residency. And of course in Africa, well, wherever they were was where he would lay his head at night, and when not sent out to the field, he was in some generic apartment in Kinshasa to which he had no attachment. Four walls and a bed, nothing more.

While Maddie's place seemed stark, her decorating style also seemed intentional, with some personally chosen pieces of art, perhaps showcased even more by the monochromatic décor. It was hard to tell since it was dark and he didn't dare turn on any lights. Bad enough he was trespassing—more like breaking and entering.

He followed some noises coming from down a hall, where he found a door wide open. A movie played on a large television mounted on the wall, and from his vantage point, he could see the corner of a bed. Well, here went nothing.

"Okay I don't want to scare you, but I'm here and I hope you don't kill me for sneaking in. It was the only way I could get to you, so please, Maddie, can we talk?" He turned the corner into the bedroom and felt something hard slam into his rib cage as he heard her scream.

"Fuck! That hurt. What the hell was that?" He rubbed his midsection.

He turned to see Maddie standing on her bed, her back up against the wall, her hands holding a pillow up to cover her body. She looked a mess: her hair disheveled, black makeup streaking her face, dark rings beneath her eyes. Clearly she'd been crying and had put any hint of self-maintenance on the back burner.

"Donovan! What the hell?" She slid back down onto the bed, her breath racing, no doubt from fear.

"Mads, I'm sorry. I didn't mean to scare you." He leaned over to pick up the remote control, which appeared to be the weapon of choice Maddie had used against her intruder. "I'd suggest you try something a little sharper next time. Oh, and you really should make sure to lock your door when you're in here alone."

She stared at him bug-eyed. "No shit, Sherlock."

"So, uh, I went to the Peg Leg tonight." This was far more awkward than he thought it would be. What do you say to someone who hates your guts after you've broken into their place? "And your trivia crew, your *T-Crew*"— he made a silly hand gesture with three fingers up on each hand like he was a rapper—"was worried about you."

"I'm sure they were fine. They could handle it without me."

He shook his head. "Not according to them. They said they do the trivia matches for fun, but you have all the answers, and that for you it's far more important. So much so that they were worried you were going to sacrifice the big state championship this weekend." He cocked his head to the side. "Congratulations, by the way. That's an impressive accomplishment. I'm proud of you. I had no idea you were such a big deal in the world of trivia competition. I didn't know it had become a vocation."

"It's not a vocation," she snapped, which didn't bode well. Snapping was never a sign of receptivity. "It's something I do to while away the time."

"Well, that's good. It's something you love and you're good at it and you're making a name for yourself."

"Yeah, until you came along and ruined it all."

Now they were making progress. This he could deal with—far better than silence.

"I'm sorry, Maddie. I didn't intend to ruin anything for you. I wish you didn't feel that way."

She pursed her lips. "Well, you did. And I do."

"I know you think I came back to ruin your life, but the truth is, I came back to find me, Maddie. I guess it's hard for you that part of finding me meant manning up to face what I did to you long ago. I'd hoped that you would be glad to get some closure about how much I hurt you—I didn't think it would make you sad and angrier. Honestly, I'm sorry."

She didn't respond, so he continued.

"Forever, my life has been out of balance. I reached a point where I knew I had to learn to dial back the intensity of what I was experiencing. I had gotten to a point where I didn't feel entitled to live a normal, happy existence knowing there was so much suffering out there. So here I went to Africa to try to figure out what was missing in me, and instead, it made me reject much of who I was or what I'd become." He reached for a cup of water on her nightstand and took a sip. "I guess it wasn't till I came home and started spending time with family— with the people who are important in life—that I allowed myself to accept that even a pampered life is not a crime. I didn't have to wallow in the notion that I should be suffering, simply because everyone else is suffering. That I can do things to help mitigate it, but it doesn't nullify my life either. It was a hard lesson to come to grips with."

He put the cup down and went on. "What I get now, and what sucks for those at the raw end of things, is it comes down to where you're born and what you do with it. For my patients in the DRC, they didn't have many choices. Most of them were stuck there with no options. For me—and for you, and for everyone we know—we have a lot more control over our lives and how we choose to lead them, for the most part." He heaved a sigh. "So how does this tie in to me and you and this?" He spread his arms out wide and continued.

"That day—right before I left for college. My father sat me down and told me I was irresponsible if I led you on. That I was moving on in my life and couldn't let you hold me back. That you would never want to hold me back, and the two-year age difference didn't matter so much when we were both in high school, but once I went to college it would be huge. He said I needed to let you down gently because it was inevitable I would dump you—it was only a matter of when, so why wait any longer?"

"I was a stupid kid who always did what my father told me to do. You saw how mean my dad could get when we didn't listen to him. I didn't have the balls to go against him. So instead, I hurt you. And for that, I hope you'll be able to forgive me at some point."

The only sounds he heard were her quiet sobs and the television on low in the background. Leaning over, he grabbed a box of tissues from her nightstand and handed her one. She blew her nose, hard. He looked over to see what she was watching. "*The Notebook*? Like you needed a reason to cry?"

She nodded. "I figured I'd get all the tears out if I kept watching this."

"You mean you've watched it more than once?"

She thrust her lower lip out in a pout. "I've had it on nonstop all day, on depression binge." She started bawling, and he handed her a steady stream of tissues while she soaked up the tears.

"So are you ready to talk to me? Tell me what's been going through that mind of yours?" He took off his shoes, then sat down on the bed next to her, leaning against the headboard and crossing one leg over the other, the heel of his foot resting on the toe of his other. "'Cause I'm not leaving till you get it all out."

"What if I don't wanna talk to you?"

He shrugged. "Pretend I'm not here. Start saying what you'd say to me if I was here, except I'm not. Even though I am."

"That doesn't even make sense."

He held up his hands. "Hey, I only have a short-lived psych rotation under my belt, so believe me when I say I'm no expert in delving into emotional turmoil. If what I say is not making sense, then take it with a grain of salt."

He looked at her, lying on the bed, looking like she'd lost her best friend, her dog, and her job all on the same day. It broke his heart to see her suffering like this, and he wasn't sure what he should do to help her. So he reached out his hand and started scratching her scalp, ever so gently, feeding her tissues as needed between her sobs. At last, she began to talk.

"I feel super stupid," she said, blowing her nose into yet another tissue. "You coming back here and seeing me for the first time at a trivia match."

He squinted his eyes. "Why would that matter that I saw you there?"

"Because." She started to wail again, and he gentled her with soft strokes on her scalp. "Trivia was the final connection I had to you. You were gone, everything was gone. But I had that link. And so I stayed with it. It became my obsession. I couldn't let it go. I got so caught up in it I established all these weird rituals that made it mine. And I know that isn't normal. Everyone else there is out with friends at a bar drinking and socializing, and I'm trying to kick their asses."

He chuckled. "Nothing wrong with taking names and kicking butt."

She pouted. "And then you came back and messed up my mojo and now I don't even know what to do. I need the money. It was going to give me a chance to do something with my life. Maybe something interesting. And yeah, it's not brain surgery—"

"You do know that I don't operate on brains, right? And that my being a doctor doesn't make me the least bit more interesting than you."

She cried out loud. "But at least it's better than working at a bed-and-breakfast." He handed her more issues.

"What is it you plan to do with the winnings?" He grinned at her. "Because we both know you're going to win."

"I want to go to pastry school. I've saved up a lot of money, but this would give me enough to do it and live off the savings without stressing about money."

"You're a baker?"

She nodded. "It's the other thing I did a lot after you left. I spent many a lonely night baking in the kitchen while Carter was out working a night job to bring in money, and my stupid father was sleeping off his liquor. There are curative powers in sugar, flour, eggs, and vanilla, you know."

"No doubt." Donovan smiled. "Look, Mads. Contrary to popular belief, I'm not your mother. Well, that goes without saying. But I know why you've paired me with her in your mind. I get it. She left. I left. To you, we're both leavers. And leavers suck. Leavers are heartless assholes. But I'm here to tell you I didn't mean to be. I should never have been. I don't know about your mom or what her motivation was. I wish I did, and I wish I could help you figure that out." He stroked his fingers through her wild mass of dark curls, bunching her hair around his fingers like he used to do when they were young.

"And I want you to know that I'm back. I'm here now, and I'm sorry. I can't begin to tell you how deeply I regret what I did to you. It was cowardly and immature… the action of a confused boy. And now I'm a clearheaded man. A man who knows what he wants and unlike that boy from so long ago, I'm not going to cower to anyone. And I'm willing to do whatever it takes to win you back, earn your love, and get you to agree to spend the rest of your life with me. I'm dead serious. And I'll spend the rest of my life proving that to you."

"I'm pretty sure 'leaver' isn't a word."

He hoped that didn't mean she'd not heard the rest of what he'd said. He smiled.

"Yup. But it worked." As he slid down and turned to his side so that he was lying facing her now, he rolled onto something sharp.

"Ouch! What's this?" He picked up a rudimentary doll that had been pressed under his rib cage, about three inches tall, with pins sticking out of it everywhere. He grinned. "Is this what I think it is?"

Maddie hung her head. "Maybe. It depends on what you think it is."

He remembered she'd kept a voodoo doll of her mother and should've assumed she'd done so with him as well. He tapped the doll with his finger. "Is this me?"

She nodded, a flush of red crossing her face. "And these are the reasons for my, let's see, headache, eye pain, groin ache, incontinence, stomach discomfort, sore ankle, and that pain in the butt that won't seem to go away?"

He began to pull the pins out, first the one in the

skull. He rubbed his head. "Amazing! My headache! It's gone! It's a miracle!" Next he pulled the one from the eye, the throat, the stomach, and the ankle. "I can see! I can swallow! I can walk! Here I am a medical expert and I never thought I'd be cured from all of this horrific pain." Finally he pulled the pin from the crotch. "Thank God I've gotten to the root of this problem. Maybe now my cock will live to see another glorious day." He pulled her hips toward his and pressed it up against her. "See, look. It's working already."

Stop," she said on a whine. "It wasn't a literal thing. It was figurative. My way of getting my anger out."

He smiled. "I understand. And I won't hold it against you. But I will hold this against you if you'll let me." He gyrated against her some more. "You know another way to purge that rage?"

She shook her head. "I'm afraid to ask."

"Makeup sex. It's been clinically proven to cure what ails you."

"I'm sure it's a weight-loss tonic that helps you sleep better at night, makes your skin radiant, and your eyes brighter too."

"I can't guarantee any of those results, but why don't we test it out to see?"

Chapter Fifteen

DONOVAN leaned over and pressed his forehead to Maddie's, then reached his tongue out to swipe along the seam of her lips. She thought she'd died and gone to heaven. But was it heaven or hell? Did she stay or did she go? Make that, should she make him leave? It seemed unavoidable. This avalanche that surely had started as a tiny sneeze of an anonymous animal in some forest far, far away had been barreling down the mountain at warp speed, and now here Maddie was, about to be buried in it or about to take cover to save herself from the inevitable.

What the hell was she supposed to do? Did she answer to her head, her heart, or her libido?

Of course Donovan was doing his part to contribute to Maddie's decision-making by skirting his hands up the ratty T-shirt she was wearing—the one with dried-up spots of chocolate ice cream on the front, but who was looking? And he somehow had managed to lift the whole thing over her head before she even knew what had happened. All while seemingly not disengaging his lips from hers, though surely he must have. All she could do was let him work his wiles on her with those lips, that mouth, pressed against hers. When his tongue wended its way into her mouth and probed along her teeth and gums and aha! finally, found her tongue, what was she to do but match him ferociously, their tongues sparring as if continuing the debate that had racked her brain since he'd shown up a week ago.

Somehow in the midst of all this, her fears seemed diminished. Because it was him—Donovan!—whose warm hands stroked along her back and worked their way to the important bits and glided along her smooth belly, then quickly found her breasts and caressed them lovingly, cherishing each one before his fingers started to focus on her nipples. And dammit, Donovan knew playing with her nipples was all it took to set her on fire—she could almost climax merely from his touch.

Their breathing had become more rapid and her heartbeat pulsed in her throat, the very throat where Donovan's tongue had worked its way down, licking and sucking as he went along her jawline, then her ears, then her throat. Now his flattened tongue stroked along her cleavage until his hands fed her nipple to his mouth, and he went wild sucking and biting and licking until Maddie's breath was panting triathlon fast.

While his mouth fastened to her breast, his hand made haste toward the waistband of her panties. For a fleeting second, she hoped he didn't notice the overstretched elastic and the hole in the seam. It wasn't like her to wear ugly underwear, but these had been trying times, and laundry had been neglected. At this point, she was lucky they were clean from today.

Thankfully Donovan's fingers had other plans and slipped with facile ease beneath the waistband and quickly found her wet center, where his fingers went to work, stroking and sliding along her slick juices, circling her clit as she moaned loudly. She had no resiliency when it came to him and his sexual maneuvers. He knew how to get to her and wasn't playing fair because all she wanted was to feel him there, right there, where his fingers played.

She gyrated her hips, encouraging him onward, and he complied, sliding two fingers inside her channel as the palm of his hand slid along her center, and his thumb toyed with her clit. They say men can't multitask, but he was proving that adage wrong, sucking and biting her nipple while his hand was perilously close to bringing her to orgasm. She wanted to feel him inside her but was too shy or too embarrassed or too caught up in how good it felt to tell him. Instead she thrust her hips toward his hand as he finger fucked her, faster and faster, until at last, she broke, her pelvic muscles contracting and shooting sparks of fire throughout her body. She shuddered with pleasure.

Their breathing was loud and ragged and soon she heard the rustling of fabric. Maddie grabbed Donovan's waistband and helped him shrug out of his sweatpants; then he was on top of her, his chest pressed to her chest, flesh to flesh, his knees spreading hers apart, his lips on her lips, their tongues entwined. His hard cock rubbed along the tip of her clit and slid through the slick moisture of her lips, and she gasped, her swollen clit still so sensitive, the sensation so amazing. The head of his cock spread her lips wide as he entered her, slowly, so slowly, as they both relished the feel of his warm, hard body joining with her soft, wet body till his cock was seated deep inside her. He let out a moan that resonated through their bodies as she clasped her legs around his back and he began to withdraw, only to plunge deep inside her again.

"I'm afraid I'm not going to last," he whispered as he planted kisses all over her face, then spread her hair out against the pillow and held her face in his hands. "I've been waiting for this moment for so long it's overwhelming me."

With that, he thrust into her hard, pulling back and pumping harder as his hand slipped between them, so he could slick his fingers along her clit and bring her to climax again. Maddie gyrated her hips against him as the sensation built up inside her again, and when Donovan froze, balls deep inside of her, his body jerking in spasms as he let out a loud shout of relief, she, too, went over the edge, her pussy clutching his hard cock, pulling the seed from deep within him, filling her up with it.

They lay with their sweat-glistening bodies pressed together, Donovan still buried inside of Maddie, their breathing slowing down. He stroked her hair and murmured into her ear before finally slipping out of her. That's when they both realized what they'd done.

"Oh shit. Condom." Maddie's voice rose in alarm.

"Oh God, Mads, I'm so sorry. I got so lost in you I completely forgot. If it helps at all, I haven't been with anyone in ages."

"I hadn't even thought about that. But what if I get pregnant! I can barely afford to take care of myself, let alone another human being."

"You mean you're not on anything?"

She shook her head. "I'm not exactly working my way through the men of Verity Beach, so, no. I hate taking medicine if I don't have to and I opted not to bother. I figured if I was planning to sleep with someone I'd cross that bridge when I came to it."

"You came to it." He smiled. "More like you came at it. Or on it."

"And you came in it. I will kill you if you make me pregnant, Donovan Reeves."

He kissed her mouth. "I dunno," he said, kissing lazy circles around her face as he spread her hair out again along the pillow. "I quite like the idea that I could put a baby in here." He reached down and stroked her belly. "You would be beautiful pregnant, your belly ripe with our child."

Fear crept along her spine. It was one thing to drop her guard to have sex with the man who she'd long viewed as her sworn enemy. But it was another thing altogether to imagine him impregnating her, which would mean, what? That they would be bound together forever with a child that was created by both of them? Maddie was so not ready for that scary notion. She wasn't even sure what her intentions were with Donovan, and now this?

She yawned and feigned exhaustion to end the discussion. Nothing good would come of it now and she needed to compartmentalize that whole ball of wax elsewhere.

Maddie woke to Donovan spreading her legs wide as his mouth descended on her pussy, and the minute his tongue stroked along her lips, she gasped with pleasure. It had been a crazy long time since anyone had done this to her and holy cow, had she forgotten how amazing it felt. But he was reminding her, as his tongue traced figure eights along her pussy and around her clit and then pressed deep inside her. It took a scant minute or two until she orgasmed. Right when she thought she couldn't come again, he shifted and settled his cock over her mouth while he continued his tongue assault on her pussy. Maddie hadn't been sure if she was ready to do this with him. It required a lot of trust to go there—at least for her it did. And it seemed like he was all ready to resume the way things had been, but was she?

She still didn't know, but it also seemed inappropriate under the circumstances to politely decline, so instead, she decided to test the waters, taking a swipe along his hard length with her tongue. He let out a joyful moan, which vibrated along her center in a very good way. Hmmm, maybe this was a better idea than she first believed. It didn't take long for her to get into it wholeheartedly—it was, she reminded herself, much like riding a bike. A long, hard, thick, pulsing one. After licking him from base to tip, she took the tip of him into her mouth and closed her lips around it, alternately sucking and licking until she moved her mouth down his length, taking him fully into her mouth.

"Ah, babe, keep going," Donovan said with a groan, and she obliged, sucking him hard as she stroked along his base with her fist. His excitement was palpable and it got her horny knowing how turned on he was. She thrust her pussy into his mouth as he pumped his length into hers. On the edge again, she convulsed in orgasm, causing her to lose focus on him as she shouted out. Quickly, he shifted away and grabbed his cock, stroking long and hard along the length of it as she joined him, their hands working together to bring him to climax. He came hard, spurting warm come onto her stomach. If they were going to continue this, they were going to need to score a box of condoms, stat. The big question was.... were they going to continue this, or was she going to bring this to a close?

Chapter Sixteen

HOW could he fucking forget condoms? What self-respecting guy didn't have a stash at the ready for these occasions? Obviously one who hadn't expected to need them, that's who. He ought to turn in his guy card and his doctor card at once for the transgression. Not that he had a doctor card, but still.

To think he could have been buried balls deep in her all night long, but no, he had to short-circuit that goal with what had to be the biggest oversight of his adult life (on top of the biggest oversight of his younger life, which was ending the relationship with Maddie as he did). Luckily they were able to be creative and managed to find other almost-as-gratifying ways to play together.

When they woke to the sun sneaking through the edges of the drawn shades, he was hoping for another chance, but it seemed Maddie had turned cold, dammit. When he stroked his hands along her body, hoping to get a response, instead he got shut down.

"Look, Donovan," she said on a deep sigh. "I still have a lot to think about. I don't know where my head is with this whole thing." She spread her arms out in demonstration.

"Maybe you're overthinking this a bit too much," he

said, hating the early morning cock-block. "Why not go with your feelings and see where it leads you?"

She shook her head. "That's what got me into this mess in the first place. I need to use logic and intelligence, not listen to my crotch."

Shit, he'd happily listen to her crotch if she'd let him.

"So where does that leave us?" He climbed out of the bed, taking the hint: persisting now would get him nowhere. God, being inside her, warm and wet, had felt incredible. And to come inside her, with nothing between them to block it, gave him an almost primal form of pleasure.

She shrugged. "I've gotta focus on this thing this weekend. When that's done, maybe we can talk."

Maybe we can talk? Was she for real? Did she truly not feel what he was feeling? A connection ten times as powerful as what they'd had when they were kids? This was the real thing, this was the lifetime thing. How could she not see that? God, what he would pay to stop her protestations and settle this the old-fashioned way: by making love until they couldn't move, their bodies so sated from pleasuring one another they had nothing left in them but sleep.

At this point, maybe he was going about this all wrong. Maybe he was being too compliant—he was pandering to her and she saw him as too easy with no challenge. Maybe he should let her think she didn't have such a solid grip on him. In truth, he wasn't going anywhere. He'd dig in until he won her over.

He tugged on his sweats that had been cast aside in a hurry last night, then rifled around for his shirt and pulled it over his head. He grabbed his shoes, figuring he'd worry about putting them on once he left her condo.

"Okay, Mads. I've said all that I can say. I guess the ball's in your court. I'm not going to bother you anymore. You're going to have to make the next move. And if you don't, well, then, I guess you can't see a future with us the way I can. I'll be sorry about that, but I know I can't force you to love me again."

He leaned over and kissed her on the forehead then turned and walked away. Leaving her this way was the second hardest thing he'd ever done. But this time she held all the power, and he only hoped she would use it to make good decisions.

Somehow the Peg Leg was defaulting into Donovan's local hangout. Perhaps it was because he hoped he'd run into Maddie, but even if he did, he'd be forced to avoid her. Pressing himself on her wasn't helping matters, so he needed to be out of sight, out of mind.

He was sitting at the bar, drinking a Sharkbite when Olivia pulled up the stool next to him.

"Hey, Donovan," she said.

"Oh hey, Liv," he said. "I can call you Liv, can't I?"

She shrugged. "Why not? I've been called worse things."

He laughed. "Can I get you a drink?" She nodded and asked the bartender for the same thing he was having. "You're not boning up for the big contest tomorrow?"

"Remember when I told you this was really Maddie's thing? I show up at them, but it's more for moral support. It's not as if I have great answers or anything. We leave all the heavy lifting to her." She took a sip of the beer the bartender had handed her. "So how'd it go the other night? Did you dazzle her with your trivia skills?"

He pursed his lips. "I'd like to say I dazzled her with some other skills but…"

"Didn't work?"

He shook his head. "Honestly I couldn't even tell you what did and didn't work. We had what I thought was yet another heart-to-heart conversation. Things went from there—"

"To more body-to-body talk?"

"Oh yeah…"

"And still she won't yield?"

"I mean, it seemed like we were having a great time and had made great progress in overcoming the emotional obstacles but then she backpedals and gets all icy on me and basically won't commit to even speaking to me, let alone having sex with me."

"You mean you two had sex?" She winked at him.

"Ugh, not only did we, but we forgot to use a condom." He raked his fingers through his hair, once again mentally berating himself for that rookie maneuver.

Olivia squinted at him. "Wait a minute. You're telling me Maddie Henderson—Maddie who never strays from the rule book. Maddie, the woman who never takes risks. Maddie, who probably hasn't touched a handrail without then using hand sanitizer for as long as I've known her—had sex with you with no protection?"

"I know, I'm sorry. It won't happen again." Of course why was he telling her this?

Olivia pushed against his arm. "Are you kidding me? This is amazing. You broke the wall, dude. You got her thinking past her fears and made her just feel. That is freaking amazing. I'm so excited for you!" She clapped her hands together. "This is so awesome."

Donovan knit his brow, confused. "You lost me."

"Trust me, if Maddie wasn't intensely into you, she would have a) not slept with you to begin with and b) made damn good and sure you were sporting a glove. For that matter, I'm sure she must've had them at her place—I wonder why she didn't demand them after the fact."

"Well, later we kind of worked around that situation."

"Oooh, so you did all sorts of fun things and didn't let the lack of protection stop you. She could've simply sent you packing, you know."

"I kind of feel like ultimately she did."

"When was that?"

"The next day."

"Meaning, you got there after we sent you, so say, seven o'clock at night. And you were there until the next morning? Honey"—she slapped his knee—"you have got her in the crosshairs. It's only a matter of time now before she breaks."

"I'm not sure if I want to break her."

"Not in that way. But you sure as hell want to break

her emotional wall down. After all, you're the one who built it, indirectly, so it's your job to tear it down."

"Yeah, she basically said, 'Don't call us, we'll call you.' So I'm not sure how I'll ever have a chance to make any more headway at this point."

Olivia stopped to plait her hair into a side braid. "Sorry, that helps me to concentrate." He nodded at her. Whatever it took. "So, tomorrow's the big competition. It's only about an hour from here. I'm supposed to drive with Maddie in the morning, but what if I come down with a nasty stomach bug? And what if I call her minutes before I'm supposed to meet her, so she can't find someone to take my place? And what if I promise I will find a replacement for her? And what if it just so happens that replacement is you?"

He tipped his head and stared at her. "You can be a devious one, can't you?"

"Sometimes the cause trumps the morals."

He broke into a broad smile. "I love your idea. A lot. It would give the two of us a chance to work together as a team and maybe she could remember how well we did work together. But…" He took a deep breath. "I'm afraid she'd shut me out. She'd say she had enough help with Tamara and Jesse."

Olivia bit her lip. "Hmmm. She does seem pretty dug in on this. I'm afraid you're right. But… what if she gets there and Jesse calls and tells them they're having car trouble and they're going to be late?"

"I'm afraid it might give her a heart attack."

"Let me ask you this: could the two of you do this together? Do you need the three of us?"

He took a swig of his beer and nodded. "Blindfolded

with my hands tied behind my back. Nothing personal."

"No offense taken." She smiled. "Then it looks like we have ourselves a plan."

"But what about the other two? Won't they be disappointed that they're missing this big event? You guys have worked so hard for it."

"Not in a million years would they care. Like I said, we do it for fun on Wednesday nights. None of us are vested in being trivia champions. We do it to help Maddie since it makes her happy."

"And you don't think she'll forfeit?"

"I think she'll be mad as a rabid fox. But I think she's too far down this path to back out now. You'll be carrying the weight of three great minds on your shoulders. You're sure you can do it?"

He gave a thumbs-up. "No question."

"In that case, Operation Land Maddie is officially underway. Synchronize your watches, ladies and gentlemen," she looked down at her cell phone. "I don't have one, so there's that. Nevertheless, I'll be calling her right before it's time to meet. She was driving anyhow, so she'll go on without me. And I'll get the other two on board, make sure they call as she's arriving with news of their car problems. Of course we'll all be there in the audience, lending moral support. But we're going to leave it to you to take care of the rest."

"If we can pull this off, Liv, I owe you one, big-time."

"If we can pull this off, make sure I'm the maid of honor at the wedding."

He smiled and winked at her. "It might take awhile for her to talk to you again, you know."

She nodded. "She's a stubborn bitch. But she'll come around. She's even doing it with you, isn't she?"

"I sure hope so. I sure hope so."

Chapter Seventeen

MADDIE was pacing the distance of her condo waiting for Olivia to arrive when her phone rang.

"Shit, Mads, you're so gonna kill me. But I can't make it. I've been throwing my guts up for the past two hours. I couldn't even stop to call you till now—it's been nonstop."

Maddie's face fell. She couldn't do this without Olivia. Impossible.

"But what're we gonna do? We didn't plan it this way. The whole thing will be messed up."

"You've still got Jesse and Tamara," Olivia said. "Plus I'm going to find a replacement for me. Mark my words, by the time you get there there'll be someone else there in my stead."

"Maybe that guy Corky would come last minute?" Maddie said, trying to think of some other regulars from the bar.

"Nope. Corky was getting married this weekend."

"Oh well, I guess he wouldn't postpone that, now would he?" Maddie squeezed the bridge of her nose with her finger and thumb. "I know—Hannah. The one who's kind of obsessed with frogs and always gets the frog-related questions right?"

"I think she moved to DC. Don't worry about it. I'll go through the teams and find the perfect replacement. I swear to you there will be a fabulous player there for you. And you know I'll be rooting for you the whole time."

Maddie ended the call and got into the car. Her stomach was jittery and she hadn't even had coffee yet. She wanted to swing by the doughnut shop and get a bunch of doughnuts and stuff them all into her mouth, but that was not in her ritual schedule, so she was not going to break with tradition.

To stave off a panic attack, she went straight to her mindful self-affirmations:

I am the architect of my life; I built its foundation and I choose its contents.

Today, I am brimming with energy and overflowing with joy.

I am superior to negative thoughts and low actions.

I have been given endless talents, which I begin to utilize today.

I possess the qualities needed to be extremely successful.

Creative energy surges through me and leads me to new and brilliant ideas.

My ability to conquer my challenges is limitless; my potential to succeed is infinite.

I am at peace with all that has happened, is happening, and will happen.

I'm the fucking queen of trivia.

Oh, but was she? She was always so good at it, but to be truthful, Donovan was way, way better than she was. If she was the queen, then he sure as hell was the king and a well-deserved title that was. Thank God he hadn't gotten back earlier in the year, or he'd be the one going to states. Not that it mattered. She wasn't going to think about him right now. Or about how amazing it felt when he made love to her and even more so when he came inside her. She'd never had someone do that before and it seemed so, well, incredibly intimate.

Shame that couldn't happen again, but no way. As much as she'd love that, she wasn't going to put herself in that position. Besides, she didn't know if she'd ever be with him again. But she had to put that out of her head— she had a competition to win, and this was a big one.

She pulled up to the Performing Arts Center at the College of The Albemarle in Elizabeth City and followed the signs toward the registration area. As she was approaching it, her phone rang.

"Maddie? It's me, Jesse."

"Please tell me you're pulling up to the parking lot right now."

"Bad news: my car broke down. We're about thirty minutes away. Waiting for a tow truck now."

"What do you mean waiting for a tow truck? Can't you hitchhike and leave the car for later?"

"It doesn't work that way. The tow truck guy said we were his second call of the day so he should be here soon. We'll get there as soon as possible, but we have to stay with him till he takes this to the closest mechanic."

"And then what, you'll find an Uber or a Lyft in East Buttfuck, North Carolina?"

Maddie's breathing became labored. Dammit, she hated when these panic attacks came on. She tried to breathe her way through it.

"We'll be there soon. Promise."

She hung up and scurried to the registration desk.

"Okay I've got you all signed in here Miss Henderson," the older man with hair sprouting from his nostrils told her. "And I see your teammate has already arrived."

She scrunched her nose. "Oh. My teammate. Would you mind telling me which one that is?"

"Looks like it says here someone named Donovan Reeves."

Maddie thought her head was going to explode. "That dirty rotten double-crosser! I'm so gonna get even with her."

The man stared at her then called for the next registrant.

She followed the signs into a large theater. On the stage were ten small tables set up for the ten finalist teams competing for the money. Her eyes scanned the horizon and there at one table, sitting alone, was Donovan. She wasn't sure who she was going to kill first, him or Olivia. She stomped her way down an aisle and up the stairs onto the stage and hissed at him.

"I need to speak with you. In private."

He got up and followed her stage left and slipped behind the large black curtain into a small prop room.

"Everything okay, Maddie?"

She glared at him. "I don't know what you are up to, but I have a sneaking suspicion you're behind this. Only I don't know how or why yet."

He ski-sloped his brows. "What are you talking about?"

She pointed at him. "You. Here. Olivia. Not.

Pretending she's sick when she's probably up and watching Saturday morning cartoons right now laughing in her Cheerios." And then she held up her phone. "And the other two."

"The other two?"

"Yes. Jesse and Tamara. Their car conveniently breaks down on the way here."

"That's a real shame. I'm sure they'll get here soon. But I'm also sure you and I will be fine without anyone else."

Just what she was afraid of: that she and he would be fine all alone. Only every time they were left alone they couldn't keep each other's clothes on.

"How is it that you of all people ended up being Olivia's replacement? For that matter, how did she even know how to reach you?"

He shrugged. "I guess Olivia put two and two together. She saw me that one time at trivia night. Then she saw me with you at the beach. She must've figured something out."

Well, crap. She'd told Olivia about Donovan and her and their trivia foreplay problem. That would teach her to confide in a good friend.

"I can't believe she sent you."

Donovan wrinkled his brow. "Why, Maddie? You and I both know I'm the best person you could have by your side today. And look, I'm going to be up front with you right now. I'm not here for anything but to help you win. I know how important it is and I know you want to get that ten thousand dollars and if—not if, *when*—we win, the money's all yours. I don't want a penny of it. I want you to be happy. Okay?"

Maddie shook her head in disbelief. "Here I worked so hard to control everything and now it's all out of my control."

"Maybe it's a sign from the universe to go with the flow."

"Universe my ass," she muttered as she turned to walk back to the stage.

Chapter Eighteen

A man named Harry Schlossberg was the emcee for the competition. Harry was about as tall as he was wide and had thick glasses that slid down his nose, forcing him to push them back up again constantly. Maddie was going to have to try hard not to focus on that, or she'd lose her cool. She needed to keep her eyes in one place: on the prize. She was queen of fucking trivia and that prize was hers.

The audience was filtering into the auditorium, and the bright lights onstage made it hard to see anyone out there, which was fine by her. She would rather not have the distractions of audience hecklers or whatever might be going on that could be distracting.

She sat down, and Donovan plunked down right next to her. Really? He couldn't be across from her? Oy.

He started pulling things out of a backpack he'd placed on the floor next to his seat.

"I got you a bottle of water," he said, placing it in front of her. "I know you prefer a certain brand and wanted to be sure you had it."

Then he reached for more. "You always loved those orange peanut butter crackers, the kind in the cellophane wrapper, so I brought you a pack. And I know you're a big fan of power bars. Or at least you used to be."

He set two power bars on the table. "I wasn't sure which brand so I got two different ones."

Now Maddie felt like a jerk for being so uptight. How thoughtful of him to do this.

"And lastly this." He pulled out one silver-wrapped Hershey's Kiss. "A kiss for good luck."

She was an ass. She should've been thanking him for taking time out of his weekend to do this with her instead of berating him.

"Thanks, Donovan. I appreciate you helping out like this. I'm sorry I was being cranky. It's only that I hate losing control."

He cocked an eyebrow, placing his hand over hers. "Huh. I hadn't noticed." He grinned, then stuck his pinkie finger in his dimple to tease her.

Harry announced the competition was about to begin, and first, he named each team. The only one she recognized was Let's Get Quizzical, a team she'd squeaked a win out of last year at some competition. When he announced the team called We Like to Come from Behind, she couldn't help but look over at Donovan—surely he still remembered that was her favorite position. Oh God. She could not start thinking about that right now! She'd be backstage with her dress up and her panties down before intermission if she went there.

Donovan grinned at her.

She'd have to deal with that later.

And when they announced the team the Cunning Linguists, well, shit. She was certain her face had turned bright red.

Of course Donovan kept a straight face, even though she knew what he was thinking, which made it all the worse.

"Ugh, I feel like throwing up right now," she said. She hadn't meant to say that aloud, but she did.

"Hey, Mads. You've got this. You're kick-ass with trivia. You know more than everyone here, and if you don't know it, I do, so I've got your back. Okay? Just start counting the winnings now."

She smiled, grateful he was trying to help settle her nerves.

Harry started with the first question: "How old is the earth estimated to be? a) 8.5 billion years, b) 1 billion years, or c) 4.5 billion years. Contestants, please settle on an answer."

"That's easy," Maddie said as she jotted down her answer and turned so Donovan could see.

"Yup."

Donovan walked the answer up when Harry asked them to turn in their answers.

"And everybody got that right," Harry said.

Next question: "In the book of Genesis, what did God create on the third day? Was it a) night and day, b) land and vegetation, c) stars, sun, and moon?"

"Not so into the biblical stuff," Maddie said. "I could hazard a guess, but what about you?"

"This is when that mandatory religious studies course from freshman year comes in handy. It's B—land and vegetation."

"You're sure about that?"

"Didn't I say I had your back?"

She smiled. It felt kind of nice, this feeling of being

able to trust him.

They hadn't gotten a question wrong yet. Maddie had to admit they made a great team. He was so good at sports and science questions, and she was excellent with pop culture and arts and entertainment.

"Which is colder?" Harry said. "Ice or water at zero degrees Celsius?"

"Oooh, I know this," Donovan said. "Ice. It has to do with latent heat."

"I'm so going to trust you with this one."

He smiled. "Thanks. I appreciate that you trust me." He squeezed her hand.

By the time intermission came along, Maddie was feeling comfortable. "Not gonna let the Cunning Linguists beat me," she said when Harry announced that they were tied in the lead with that team.

"Oh, I don't know," Donovan said. "I think that you and I and the Cunning Linguists could be a winning combination." He winked at her and she smacked his arm playfully.

Which got her to thinking about the last time she and Donovan had a halftime break in the action. She definitely couldn't do that this time. Even though watching him in action made the heat build inside her. The man was smart. And smart was super sexy to her.

They were in the pop culture rounds now. Harry had asked what was Elton John's first US hit. Choices were: a) Goodbye Yellow Brick Road, b) Crocodile Rock, or c) Rocket Man.

"My brother played that music till my ears bled. I'm sure it's Crocodile Rock," Maddie said.

"I trust you, babe."

"Thanks, Donovan." She smiled.

"What was blond bombshell Jayne Mansfield's IQ measured at? Was it a) 175, b) 120, or c) 163?" Howie asked the contestants.

"Oh crap. I know we've had this question before. But I can't remember it," she said. "Any clue?"

"Let's go for the middle number. I think it's the best guess in a situation like this."

And once again he got it right. So far they hadn't gotten an answer wrong.

It was the final question before the bonus round. They were tied with the Cunning Linguists. Getting this answer would be helpful to go into the bonus round.

"What were Queen Elizabeth and Prince Philip of the UK given as a present for baby Prince Andrew while on a visit to the Gambia? Was it a) a baby crocodile, b) a baby chimpanzee, or c) a hippo?"

"Why the hell would they want any of those as a baby gift?" she said with a laugh.

"I'd like to think it's a chimpanzee, but that seems too obvious. And a hippo, well, they grow fast and they're dangerous."

"So's a crocodile, in case you didn't get the memo."

"I lived in Africa. I am well aware of the dangers of crocodiles."

"Did you ever treat anyone with a crocodile bite?"

"I think you're usually drowned before the bites become the problem."

She winced. "Really?"

He nodded. "They might get you with one big bite, but that's to get a good grip on you to pull you under. Then it's all over."

"Well then surely they wouldn't give a crocodile as a gift."

"Except that a three-ton hippo could just as easily bite you in half. They're big, they're strong, and they're fast."

"Okay, so we think it's a crocodile because?"

"It's a baby, won't grow that fast. It'll give them awhile to figure out what to do with it."

She shrugged and held up her hands in abandonment. "It's all yours. I haven't a clue."

When Harry announced the winners of that round, it was team Trivia Newton John.

It was the last question of the bonus round. If they got this, they won it all. Maddie could barely keep her peanut butter crackers in her stomach, she was so riddled with anxiety.

"The final question in the bonus round is as follows," Harry announced. "In what country did the 2014 outbreak of Ebola virus that led to nearly five thousand deaths begin? Was it a) Sierra Leone, b) Guinea, or c) Liberia?"

Donovan's eyes lit up. He leaned forward and whispered to Maddie.

"I know this. Patient Zero was a toddler in Guinea. Technically the child died in December of 2013. Most of the kid's family was dead by January 2014, and it quickly spread to other villages and towns and soon to Sierra Leone and Liberia."

"Wow. You are a fount of all knowledge."

"Even more so as there's another dangerous outbreak in the DRC, where I lived for a year. Pandemic experts are fearful of it spreading quickly because it's already reached Mbandaka, a city of a million people."

Maddie knit her brows. Jesus, how petty had she been, being all "boo-hoo, woe is me" with him when he was busy facing real-world fears that mattered. Not piddling emotional hangover bullshit as she had. Donovan wasn't the child who left her. He was a man who carried the weight of many on his shoulders and wanted to have her by his side to do so. How could she not have seen this before? God, if she could, she would pin him down right now and strip off his clothes and fuck him stupid.

She handed him the paper. "You do the honors, babe." She leaned over and kissed his cheek. Donovan walked the answer up to the emcee when he prompted them to, and with a drumroll, the scores were read.

"With a total of 150 points, the high score of the state championships goes to Trivia Newton John."

The crowd started cheering wildly, and Donovan returned to the table as Maddie took a running leap for him, wrapping her arms around his neck and her legs around his waist. She reached up and their lips met. The world disappeared for Maddie and all she could see was this man she almost let slip through her fingers. The applause started to die down and she realized that maybe she needed to hop down. She did so reluctantly and wiped her mouth to make sure it wasn't slobbery.

"If team Trivia Newton John could please come forward," Harry called out.

Donovan reached for Maddie's hand and they walked together to the podium.

"First, congratulations on this big win. You get to walk away with this check for ten thousand dollars!" He handed them an oversized check and they posed for pictures with it.

"And I was told there was one more special question that I had to ask, so if you'll please bear with me while I put my glasses on again." He padded around his chest pocket and then found them in the pocket of his pants. He put them on. "Okay, here it is. 'Would Maddie Henderson, proud winner of the North Carolina State Trivia Quiz, possibly find it in her heart to accept Donovan Reeves back into her life? And if so would she a) agree to forgive him, b) agree to marry him, and c) agree to live happily ever after with him?'"

Donovan got down on one knee and pulled a ring from his suit jacket pocket. Maddie stood there with her hands on her face, stunned.

"Maddie, I know I was a world-class jerk and I'm so sorry I did that to you. But I hope I've been able to prove to you that I'm back for good now, and I will always have your back. Please, will you make me the happiest man in the world, and let me make you the happiest woman in the world, by saying you'll marry me?"

Maddie looked into those brown eyes and her heart melted... as if it hadn't already.

She held out her left hand. "Well, what the hell are you waiting for, babe? Put that thing on me!"

Donovan slipped the emerald-cut emerald set in a diamond band onto her ring finger. He stood up and wrapped Maddie in a tight embrace. "I love you so much, Mads. I don't ever want to be apart from you again. With you, I've found my home."

"I'm sorry I made you suffer so much," she said between kisses.

"I'm sorry I made you suffer so much," he said. "Let's agree to put an end to needless suffering, okay?"

Through her tears, Maddie saw Olivia and Tamara and Jesse and even Carter and his girlfriend Jamie rush the stage.

She made a pretend fist and shook it at her friend Olivia. "Olivia Singletary I was so going to make you pay for what you did today, but now I realize that I owe you everything for helping me find my way back to Donovan." She gave her friend a hug. "And I hope you don't mind, guys, but you've been supplanted by my life partner, so no more me making you guys play trivia games every week."

"And I think we'll be retiring at the top of our game," Donovan said, then whispered into her ear, "except at home when we can have our own little games of trivia foreplay." Maddie blushed.

"Oh thank God," Jesse said with a laugh. "We've been hoping for the day you'd set us free."

"And I've been hoping for the day she'd tie me up," Donovan said with a laugh.

Maddie scrunched her nose. "I didn't know you were into that sort of thing."

He laughed. "I only mean that you and I are bonded for life. And at last, we can have our happily ever after."

Thank you so much for reading *Falling for Mr. Right*! I hope you enjoyed it! If so, please help others find this book:

1. Help other people find this book by writing a review.

2. Sign up for my new releases email so you can find out about the next book as soon as it's available and get fun giveaways.
   http://eepurl.com/baaewn

3. Like my Facebook page.
   www.facebook.com/jennygardinerbooks

And I love to hear from readers! Let me know what you think about my books! You can write to me at jenny@jennygardiner.net, and visit me on the web at www.jennygardiner.net.

Keep reading for a sample from *Skirt Chaser*, the first book in the all new *Confessions of a Chick Magnet* series.

Skirt Chaser

By

Jenny Gardiner

Chapter One

Twenty Year's Earlier

TANNER Eliasson was a lonely boy. The only child of film star Gina LeFevre and legendary director Brady Cox, he generally came as an afterthought to his busy—and self-absorbed—parents. Particularly to his father, who was old enough to be his grandfather, and never seemed to express much interest in Tanner except to impart annoying aphorisms that he must have thought were sage words of wisdom but instead came across as judgmental insults.

"Man up, son," he'd say if Tanner complained about just about anything. "If your only tool is a hammer, every problem looks like a nail."

Tanner didn't even know what the fuck that meant, but he chalked it up to his father being an old man with nothing better to say to a little kid.

His mother, well, she wanted to at least appear to be a loving mother, but the one his mother loved the most was herself. And boy, was she good at that. And unless Tanner wanted to spend an inordinate amount of time with his mother and her vast staff of primpers and fawners—usually spearheaded by her stylist, Eliza Fink, and her personal trainer, Jackson Mandelay, oh and her publicist, Orion Something-or-Other (Tanner could never remember if that was really her name but it was the best he could remember)—he didn't get much "me time" with his mom. Because she was always prepping for something, be it a role, or prepping to audition for a role, or prepping for an awards ceremony or prepping her body to be ready to prep for an audition or an awards ceremony. He learned early on that it took a lot of time out of your day being beautiful, and his mother was indeed beautiful. Tall, statuesque and blonde, she was pleased at least that she passed on her half-French, half - Scandinavian beauty to her only child. Daily she would stroke his flaxen locks and remark on how handsome he was, thanks to her. He grew to be embarrassed by his looks simply because it felt like his mother was complimenting herself when she praised him. Besides, he wanted to be appreciated for who he was, not how he looked.

Tanner didn't spend much time with his folks, but he also didn't spend much time with much of anyone but himself, with the exception of his beloved yellow Labrador, Sunshine. He knew from the endless gushing of strangers that he lived a charmed life—outsiders looking in were inherently jealous of his world, what with the mansion he lived in in the Hollywood Hills, complete with retractable glass walls that overlooked all of Los Angeles. Capped off with an infinity pool the color of twilight, built right into the cliffs, sure, it looked like a great place to live. But the place was overly large and lacking in soul, especially since he was usually there alone with just staff.

In fact, he was far from what few peers he had at

school. And his parents were never around to take him to play dates. His parents both had drivers, but they were driving them places, not him. And that cliff thing? He lost a pet iguana over the side of the pool deck one day, never to be seen again, so there was no charm in teetering on the edge of infinity, if it meant your pets dying on you with one false move.

When his father was home, he usually locked himself inside of his office, and would usually holler at Tanner if he "disturbed his creative genius." His mother? Well, mostly she was on location, but if not there, she was at the gym, or at some designer's studio having a fitting for another big event.

Occasionally things livened up at his house. His parents were known to throw raucous parties. Sometimes his mother's actress friends would bring their kids along, so then Tanner would get thrown in with a relative stranger and told to entertain him, but stay away from the swimming pool where the grown-ups were. The kids would usually go down the home theater and watch cartoons for a while. Then they'd go to the kitchen to see if cook could whip up some food for them. But the caterers would shoo them away, muttering about them being underfoot.

Once his parents' friends Alexa and Armando Lipari showed up at a party with their daughter, Zoey Richards. In Hollywood, lots of kids of celebrities didn't share their parents' names since they had to take on stage names. Zoey was a scrawny, brown-eyed tomboy-looking thing with a pair of dirt-stained jeans full of holes at the knees and long, brown hair that hung halfway down her back. Without so much as an introduction, her parents dumped the girl at Tanner's bedroom door with instructions to keep her entertained. Tanner rolled his eyes. What did a ten-year-old boy do with a nine-year old girl? Ugh.

"I don't know what you like to do," he said with a shrug. "I've got some Legos. Or we can watch TV. Maybe the caterers will be serving something that's not disgusting and we can mooch some of it."

She walked over to the dog sitting on the floor near the bed, and petted it.

"I like your dog," she stroked her ears as she spoke. "What's her name?"

"Sunshine," he said.

She looked skyward, as if lost in thought. "That's a good name. She seems cheery."

"Yeah, well, she is."

She frowned, then hopped up onto his bed, swinging her legs as she spoke. "I want to swim."

Tanner shook his head. "Oh, no," he said. "My parents would freak if we went to the pool. I've been told I'm not to bring anyone out to the pool during these parties, so I don't."

She furrowed her brow. "Do you always listen to what your parents tell you to do?"

Tanner thought about it for a minute. Weirdly, yeah. It just seemed to be what he did. Maybe because they weren't even really around, so it's not like there were a ton of rules. If they were out of town, he kind of just wandered the house and ate potato chips for dinner or went to bed when he wanted to. A driver would show up to take him to school, and another driver would show up to take him home at the end of the day. Every now and then he'd get a call from one of his parents—usually his mom—and always it was a call placed by her assistant.

"Hold for your mother," Eliza would say.

Then his mom would get on the phone while fielding a few other conversations in the background, she'd make a few loud smooching sounds and say she loved him, then hang up. Sometimes Tanner felt like he was living a movie scene of a life instead of a real one.

"I guess I do what my parents tell me to do," he said, frowning. "Don't you?"

She rolled her eyes. "Please. My parents hardly set the example of how one should behave in the world anyhow. Between the two of them they've had at least three lovers in the past two years, all of whom come and go as if they're our roommates. My mother's latest, some personal trainer named Georgio, comes down to breakfast in his underwear. I'm pretty sure my father is sleeping with our cleaning lady's daughter. Every time she's at the house, his hands are all over her body."

Tanner could hardly believe what he was hearing from her mouth. How could a girl her age even know of such things? Granted, kids in Hollywood tended to grow up faster than your average kid, in, say, Milwaukee. But geeze, he wouldn't have a clue if his parents were doing things like that.

"C'mon," she said, hopping off the bed and reaching for his hands. "Let's sneak into the pool."

"I'm telling you we'll get in trouble."

She grinned. She had a nice smile. "Trouble is my middle name."

Tanner heaved a deep sigh and relented. Somehow he knew this girl was not going to take no for an answer.

He led her down a long corridor that bypassed the

more public areas of the house. He didn't want to run into his parents who might put a stop to their plans.

"Do you have a swim suit?" he asked her.

She shook her head. "I'll just go in in my clothes."

"Really? Won't you be uncomfortable?"

"My motto is 'get comfortable with being uncomfortable'."

Tanner thought that was a weird thing for the child of film stars to say. He figured that like him, the one thing she would have counted on with regularity was being as comfortable as humanly possible. At least physically, if not emotionally.

They slipped down a flight of steps used mostly by the household staff and into the warm night air. They could hear loud squeals and giggles around the back of the house.

"There's no way they're not going to notice us," Tanner said, frowning. He hated to defy his parents—he knew his father would lecture him about his failure to listen to directions.

"Look," Zoey said. "Can you hear the crowd out there? There have to be at least a hundred people there. You think anyone's going to notice us? And if they do, it's not like we'll run into our parents. It'll be some strangers we don't even know. It'll be fine." She swatted at his arm. "Live a little. Have some adventure."

They turned the corner and suddenly Tanner grabbed Zoey's wrist and pulled her behind the stately-manicured bushes. He gasped loudly and quickly put his hands over her eyes.

"What the hell are you doing?" She flailed against his hands, which were pressed firmly against her face.

"Let go!" She used both of her hands to peel one of his away from her eye.

But by then Tanner was rendered speechless.

"Oh, my god," Zoey said, her mouth opened wide as she pointed at what was in front of them: a thicket of men and women—there had to have been at least fifty or so—completely naked. Some milling about, others engaged in conversation, and others still, doing things with one another that Tanner had to assume even the street-smart Zoey didn't know quite what it was.

The two of them stood stock-still, mouths agape, as they watched what Tanner would soon learn was known as an orgy unfolded before their very eyes. And the two of them nearly screamed in shock when they saw their parents pairing off with people who were decidedly not their partners.

It took a few minutes for him to regain his composure but quickly he reached for Zoey and grabbed for her, pulling her toward the house. Luckily she complied and they practically stampeded over one another to get far, far away from whatever it was those very naked, very noisy, and very creepy people were doing.

"If you ever let one person know about this, I'll never speak to you again," Tanner said, out of breath from running up the stairs so quickly.

"Fine," Zoey said. "Because I never want to see you or your parents or this house ever again." She stormed out of the bedroom and sat in the hallway the rest of the night, refusing to discuss anything. When her parents came for her she was asleep in front of his door and they asked no questions, which was fine by him.

He could barely believe what he'd seen, and the last thing he ever wanted to do, ever, was discuss anything to do with it, ever again. Thank goodness he wasn't going to have to be around that pushy Zoey Richards ever again, too.

Chapter Two

Twenty Years Earlier

ZOEY never quite felt like she fit in in her parents' world. They were all glamor and drama and paparazzi flashbulbs and she was more swing-from-the-monkey-bars-and-fall-of-and—break-a-wrist, or better yet scale the ridiculously tall fence that surrounded their imposing Malibu mansion and scrabble down the rocks to the beach, far below. Their world had never interested her.

And after that horrible night at that kid Tanner's place, god, she wanted nothing to do with her parents. Whatever they were taking part in was nothing she wanted to know about. Seeing those men with those things sticking out from between their legs about made her scream. And the women, with freakishly huge boobs that looked like Macy's Thanksgiving Day Parade floats. Yeesh. Her chest was as flat as an ironing board so she couldn't relate to that and honestly, that stuff just scared her. If she ever grew something like that she'd about die. It was as if they'd walked in on some Monster's Ball. Only Monsters would probably at least be covered in fur or something. Not naked with that icky thing sticking out. Yuck.

Tonight her folks were forcing her to go to some

stupid movie premier, which she totally didn't want to do. Her mother's stylist had shoved some annoying prissy dress on her and even stuck a bow in her hair plus swiped on lipstick—lipstick, of all things!—and she felt like an idiot. Besides she had two skinned knees so everyone would know she wasn't a dress-up kind of girl anyhow, so what was the point?

These movie premiers were the worst—she felt like an animal at the zoo. Her parents put on their acting faces, and slathered her with false affection for the cameras as they stood in front of the step and repeat banner—the one with the movie name repeated like wallpaper that the stars of the film stood before while photographers took a million and one pictures of them pretending to want to be there.

Zoey had been doing these things since she was a baby—her mother called them dog and pony shows. Although she felt more like Koko the Gorilla, with everyone pointing at them and popping off pictures like she was some freak exotic animal.

She never paid attention to whatever her parents were starring in. This was a business in her family and she was really kind of a prop for them, to be honest. It was good business for them to appear to be kind, warm, loving parents, and since they were talented actors, they did a good job of pulling that off.

Her mother held her hand and her father had his arm wrapped around her mother as they walked toward the banner. And that's when she saw him—Tanner, the kid she saw their naked parents with. The boy she never ever wanted to see again because it made her want to throw up thinking about what they'd seen together and it was beyond embarrassing. How was she to know his parents were involved with this stupid movie?

The sound of the crowds gathering for the premier grew louder in her ears. Or maybe it was her heart beating harder, pumping the blood through her veins too fast. The whole thing was just so awful. She couldn't look at his parents without seeing them stark naked, his dad with that, that, that *thing* sticking out like it did. His mother with some man's hands on her private parts like he was petting a dog.

Her mother guided Zoey up to the banner and damn if she wasn't stuck standing right next to Tanner, which was just making it all the worse. She knew her face must be the color of that tomato sauce Mr. Puck always made just for her when her parents dragged her to Spago's for dinner.

She tried to pretend Tanner wasn't there but then the photographers were telling them to hold hands and god, no, she could not touch him. His father's icky thing had been sticking out at the swimming pool. It was all so awful. Tanner was reaching for her hand—he told her he always followed the rules—and she kept trying to shake her hand away, like she had to get some gunk off of it, but the photographers were insisting.

"Zoey, grab the boy's hand," her mother said with one of those fake smiles that said, "I'm going to spank you with a wooden spoon so hard your butt is going to be too sore to sit on", while telling the cameras she was the best mother on the planet.

Just as Tanner's hand made contact with hers, Zoey just couldn't help herself. She drew back her right arm, as if she'd actually done this before, even though she hadn't, then she pivoted her body, putting the full force of herself into it, and *ka-pow*, her nine-year-old fist made contact with Tanner's nose and she heard a loud gasp and her fist hurt so badly and then he screamed out and her mother grabbed her by the arm so hard she thought it would be dislocated at the shoulder.

And then Tanner was crying: loud, aching sobs, and he was clutching on to his mother, and his nose was bleeding, and Zoey was being dragged away like a rag doll, but she could see him crying and bleeding and she felt badly but she couldn't help herself, it was all so awful. And she kept hearing him cry.

When the reviews came out the next day her father was reading the paper over breakfast, and looked up over the top edge of the paper while she moved a soggy bite of pancake around in a puddle of syrup.

"I don't know what you were thinking, young lady," he said to her in that stern voice that dads used to scare children. "But that was unacceptable behavior." He then turned to look at her mother and winked. "That said, you did us all a bit of a favor. Because we knew this movie would bomb at the box office, but as they say, no such thing as bad publicity. You'll probably bring thousands more people to the theaters to see this stinker with that bizarre little maneuver of yours."

Her mother laughed, a tinkly little laugh that made her sound like the ingénue she wanted the world to think she was.

She felt horrible for what she'd done to Tanner. But she had no way to even apologize to him. This would be the first of many lessons on why she wasn't cut out to be the daughter of movie stars.

Chapter Three

ANONYMITY was Tanner Eliasson's most prized possession. Which was saying a lot, because he owned a stunning home on a ranch with a commanding view of the snowcapped peaks of the Rocky Mountains in northwest Montana, where sunsets cast a fire of blaze-orange along the mountain range so breathtaking, you'd want to cry. He was a stone's throw away from pristine lakes and hundreds of miles of spectacular hiking and biking trails that probed deep into the Montana wilderness. In the winter he could be on the slopes in ten minutes. In the summer, he often took a brisk sail before breakfast and was back in the office in time for a full workday.

But being able to be him, not subservient to his less-than-charming past, well, he couldn't put a price tag on that. Tanner had made the decision long ago to sever ties with Tanner Cox, son of the famous film star Gina LeFevre and revered director Brady Cox. As soon as he was old enough to finally shake off the suffocating confines of his parents' fame and fortune, he took off, first for college, then vet school and finally, here, to Montana, where he could just be himself, no pretenses, no hiding from mockery, and no longer frozen out beneath the long shadow cast by his parents' larger-than-life world.

He'd even gone so far as to drop his surname, substituting instead his middle name, Eliasson. He figured no one would put two and two together to link him with that part of his life that he just really didn't have any interest in revisiting.

Every so often Tanner would reflect on that dark past of his, if only to take a deep breath and relish that he was living the opposite kind of existence now: not a reporter, no paparazzi, no film studio machine to orchestrate his behavior, nothing.

He'd certainly not enjoyed the trappings of fame. Not one bit. And things only got worse on that fateful night when that damned girl, Zoey Richards—he'd never forget her name—up and cold-cocked him in front of the cameras at the premier of his father's latest drama. Jesus, things went to shit fast after that happened. First off, it hurt like a son of a bitch—who knew a nine-year-old could punch like that? He should've known—she was such a tomboy. But then, man: his face throbbed, his nose was gushing like a damned fire hydrant, he did the first thing you do when something unexpectedly awful happens to you—you seek comfort from someone you hope will comfort you.

In his case this was his mother, who he would be sad to realize was actually upset that his blood was ruining her designer gown she'd chosen just for this special evening. Pretty quickly a cadre of studio lackeys swarmed them all, mostly to try to salvage her gown, but one underling had the presence of mind to stick some cocktail napkins underneath his nostrils to staunch the blood flow. It had been so embarrassing to be crying like a girl in front of all of those cameras, but he learned quickly that his father was even more mortified than he was.

"Stop crying or I'll give you something to cry about," he'd hissed into Tanner's ear. Tanner sobbed a little longer and stopped except for a few gasping sighs here and there.

That was the day that Tanner decided he would man-up, just like his father had so wanted him to. No more tears, no more emotion, no more nothing. Shame it was too late—the next morning the tabloids had given him his own moniker: the Weeping Wimp. Another headline read *Teary Tanner*. Nowhere did Zoey get called out for decking him for no good reason. Instead Tanner carried the shame for having done nothing but shown up at his father's stupid film premier, and it would take him years to live down the shame from that night.

Skirt Chaser

Coming September 4, 2018

About the Author

Jenny Gardiner is the author of #1 Kindle Bestseller *Slim to None* and the award-winning novel *Sleeping with Ward Cleaver*. Her latest works are the *It's Reigning Men* series, the *Royal Romeos* series, the *Falling for Mr. Wrong* series and her upcoming *Confessions of a Chick Magnet* series. She also published the memoir *Winging It: A Memoir of Caring for a Vengeful Parrot Who's Determined to Kill Me,* now re-titled *Bite Me: a Parrot, a Family and a Whole Lot of Flesh Wounds*; the novels *Anywhere but Here*; *Where the Heart Is*; the essay collection *Naked Man on Main Street*, and *Accidentally on Purpose* and *Compromising Positions* (writing as Erin Delany); and is a contributor to the humorous dog anthology *I'm Not the Biggest Bitch in This Relationship*.

Her work has been found in Ladies Home Journal, the Washington Post, Marie-Claire.com, and on NPR's Day to Day. She was also a columnist for Charlottesville's Daily Progress for over a decade, and is the Volunteer Coordinator for the Virginia Film Festival.

She has worked as a professional photographer, an orthodontic assistant (learning quite readily that she was not cut out for a career in polyester), a waitress (probably her highest-paying job), a TV reporter, a pre-obituary writer, as well as a publicist to a United States Senator (where she first learned to write fiction).

She's photographed Prince Charles (and her assistant husband got him to chuckle!), Elizabeth Taylor, and the president of Uganda. She and her family and menagerie of pets now live a less exotic life in Virginia.

Visit Jenny at her website at www.jennygardiner.net where you can sign up for her newsletter, visit her blog, or find her on Facebook and Twitter. And every blue moon she'll post adorable pictures of her pets on Instagram as @thejennygardiner.